I0638597

THINGS THAT ARE BROKEN

VIRGINIA YOUNG

Riverhaven Books

www.RiverhavenBooks.com

Things That are Broken is a work of fiction. While some of the settings are actual, any similarity regarding names, characters, or incidents is entirely coincidental.

Copyright© 2020 by Virginia Young
.

No part of this work may be used without permission of the author with the exception of book reviews and articles.

All rights reserved.

Published in the United States by Riverhaven Books, Massachusetts.

ISBN 978-1-951854-08-9

Designed by Stephanie Lynn Blackman
Whitman, MA

Also by Virginia Young

Novels

Out of the Blue

Sleepless Tides

I Call Your Name

Where Seagulls Sleep

Annasheeva

By a Thread

The Birthday Gift

Winter Waltz

A Family of Strangers

A Midnight Bell

close to you

Stone

Keeper of the Stars

Short Story Collection

Find Me

Young Adult Novel

Nocturnal

Children's Book

Mary's Goat

For more about Virginia Young and her books, please visit her
website: www.VirginiaYoung-SouthShoreWriter.com

Suzanna

"Do you hear the flowers singing?" she asked in a soft, clear voice, her wispy silver-white hair lifting in the summer wind from the sides of her straw hat.

We sat in weathered Adirondack chairs, a tall grass meadow and then the sea before us. I looked at her and then toward the swaying pink cosmos. I smiled intentionally, plotting to be receptive to her words, even if at times they ceased to make sense.

"Perhaps," I said.

She glanced at and then away from me, toward the baby blue water flirting with the shore. We were silent for several minutes, our eyes squinting to fight the glare of brilliant afternoon light.

"Would you like more lemonade?" I asked in an attempt to dispel silence. I reached for the pitcher on the small table between us.

"I think not," she said, "but thank you."

Again we were divided in thought and I wondered what she might ask next, or declare. I had hoped our visit would be flowing, easy, yet I found it tight, crisp.

"Will you be leaving this evening?" she asked.

I was surprised by the question; I hadn't anticipated her memory recalling my departure, her mind often seeming adrift.

"Yes, I'll be catching a flight back to California tonight." I'd been at her beloved Cape Cod home for three days, an eternity it seemed, courting a distracted mind, recalling both her brilliance and her determination to raise a freethinking child into an invincible yet graceful woman. I believed I had failed her.

Devoid of speech, moments turned to minutes, minutes to nearly an hour as clouds began to shield the sun. She stood, wrapped a light shawl around her shoulders, and with one last glance to the ocean, she said, "We should go in. It's all over now."

* * *

Back home in the California hills, I sip coffee while staring out at the redwoods, watching the birds as they dart limb to limb. I wonder what my trip to the Cape had accomplished other than burdening me with a heavy sense of guilt, knowing that my mother, alone for the last eight years, was likely feeling the pangs of solitary life. She never said. After forty-seven years of marriage, it must have been an adjustment. Perhaps that was why at eighty-two she was independently living at the beach house. She'd sold the old brownstone in Jamaica Plain – without consulting me, without consulting anyone else. My father would have balked at the idea of living so isolated. The city life had been more agreeable to him – public transportation, culture.

Wilted from the trip, my thoughts turn to my own nest. Glenn, my work-dedicated husband, who had traveled to Japan for business. My twenty-nine-year-old son living with another man in New Mexico. My twenty-six-year-old daughter living in New York City. I had mentioned to her that I could spend a day or two with her while East. She advised me to wait for another time – her work was keeping her busy.

I place the cup in the sink and walk into the living room to sit down in Glenn's recliner. I pull the lever at the side and lean back, closing my eyes to daylight, recalling how our Siamese cat Sienna had always come to sit with me when she heard the recliner being adjusted. She had nearly nineteen years with us – I missed her, yet hadn't braved the urge to get another.

Could you replace love?

I wasn't sure. I thought of giving another cat a good life, that I would grow to love that new offer of hope and companionship, but something held me back. Opening my eyes, I will myself to be calm, to stop thinking of what I'd lost and what I did not understand. I try to focus on my breathing, on positivity, on being glad to be alive.

Having closed my eyes at some point, I slept and woke to darkness. Glenn hadn't called. He was probably having dinner with a client. I look around the room; one dim light is on by a window where my floor-to-ceiling rubber tree plant flourishes. I'd bought that plant when it was barely eight inches high, the first of our thirty years of marriage. I said it was our baby and had named it Claire. Glenn laughed then.

Weeks later I told him we were having a baby. He asked if it was another rubber tree plant. My smile faded to a brief feeling of disappointment. No, I explained, we were having a child, a real baby. Glenn had looked startled, but eventually he smiled and commented that we might consider clearing out one of the spare rooms we'd filled with wedding presents to make space for a crib. Close to my delivery time, I did that, alone.

Glenn was away, and it had to be done. We'd discovered we were having a boy so I bought pale blue paint and turned the tan walls into the color of the sky. I ordered a white crib and changing table that doubled as a three-drawer dresser. I bought a small rocking recliner, too, white with a royal blue cushion.

When Glenn came home from his trip, I was excited to show him the baby's room. He nodded and said I'd done a good job.

Giving birth to Jordan changed everything for me. I had thought Glenn would be a hands-on father, but he rarely picked up his son and almost never played with him. No tossing a baseball in the back yard, no teaching him to ride a bike. I did those things.

When he was six, I noticed that Jordan seemed to prefer drawing or playing with his new sister, Kira. It also became evident that Jordan loved music – he wanted to learn how to play the piano. We bought an inexpensive one to see how serious he was about this new interest. He excelled, and then went on to a college noted for graduating successful musicians. It was that talent that had taken him to New Mexico for a concert where he met his love Michael, a violinist.

I broadened my thoughts to Kira. She had been a quiet child, seemingly reluctant to find an interest in anything in particular. She was incredibly smart like her father, always ready to correct me when it came to a historical fact. I was proud of her intelligence, her ability to comprehend technical aspects of life which had regularly blown my mind. I laughed at her for the knowledge she possessed, yet as she matured I found her more annoyed with my sense of humor than I'd hoped. I stopped laughing – I stopped smiling – I decided that briefly complimenting her for her achievements was my best bet.

Glenn was the same, and I found myself living alone. I understood that while there were warm bodies dwelling in my house, I had no connection to any one of them – I was the freak amidst three other humans determined to lead themselves away from everything with which I felt familiar. Running a social services office in my town, I was efficient, nothing went unnoticed or undone, but I sometimes wondered if I'd have been better at being an investigator – making certain that children placed in foster care had a positive life experience. So many of them didn't. On the other hand, maybe I was best suited to exactly what I was doing. After all, how successful was I with my own husband and children?

Adjusting the recliner so that I can stand up and stretch, I walk to the kitchen. I'm hungry but nothing I have in the house holds appeal. I wonder when Glenn will call and if he's coming home within the next day or so. I guess he'd tell me when he calls. Since it's just after eight, I make toast and spread the strawberry jam I'd bought on the Cape over the top of one slice. I heat more coffee in the microwave and sit at the kitchen island where my thoughts return to my mother. Surely she was in bed by now; it was after eleven on the East Coast.

I wondered what she'd had for dinner. While I was there with her, she was fairly agreeable to anything in food. I made salads, bought clam chowder, urged her to go with me to have seafood, clams, scallops, haddock, with a baked potato. I scrambled eggs in the morning, made coffee, and washed a kitchen window while the coffee machine gurgled and sputtered. I couldn't help wondering what she lived on. The refrigerator held scattered fruits washed and in bowls. There was always a good loaf of bread – sometimes rye, sometimes sour dough. There were jams and small containers of yogurt. It was all healthy, but not much of a meal.

Now, here I am, doing the same, eating toast with jam – definitely not a meal, but enough to appease my stomach. So, is this how it was with my mother?

I think about her often. I hadn't found her to be the type who hugged me as a child – she seemed intent on raising me to be sturdy, brave enough to face the world, and when I decided on college in California instead of Boston she appeared stunned. Dad thought it was an independent decision, a sound idea, but Mother grew quiet, said nothing discouraging or encouraging. She prepared me with a shopping trip for new clothes, bought me two new suitcases, and set up a bank account where I could withdraw funds for books and a midnight pizza. I'd felt released.

And after a few months, I'd met Glenn. We lived together until after I graduated. My parents wouldn't have approved of that arrangement had they known, but since they only visited once after my marriage, they never knew. Glenn had been a year ahead of me.

When I went home after graduation, I told my parents I was getting married. They tried subtle persuasion with the hope of turning my thoughts to remaining single for a few years. Nothing worked – I married and found myself living on the West Coast when I'd always thought I'd be a resident of Boston or its surrounding towns. I had enjoyed the city's night life and easy maneuvering on subways and buses. I shake my head, wondering why my mother chose to give all of that up.

Why do my thoughts always go back to my mother? Does that happen with other women? I had never wanted to be her – I wanted to pave my own way, and I did. Visiting with her every summer since Dad died gave me reasons to be glad I was three-thousand miles away, and then I always ended up feeling guilty for being silently

7

critical of her behavior. We'd lost our connection to one another somewhere back in my childhood. It was as if she was living in her own realm, hoping I would follow.

I didn't though – I didn't want my mother's life. Her work as a textbook editor always seemed to keep her interested and rarely available. It was a quiet house to grow up in – that fact stands out in my memory. She must enjoy the quiet. She's chosen to isolate, to be alone these eight years since my father passed. It was as if I was disturbing her tranquility – she seemed less captivated with my visit than I had expected. I wonder if her mind is clouding – her words to me had been vague.

Sadearah

I suppose Suzanna is glad to be back home in her ultra-modern house in the forest. It's a pretty place, that's for certain, but too far from the ocean, too darkened by tall, gorgeous old redwoods. We visited there once, Henry and me, and I couldn't wait to be right back here, the salt air teasing my senses, the sand beneath bare feet. Henry preferred the city offerings, but he was always agreeable to a weekend at the Cape.

We found our way through forty-seven years, one child, and two fulfilling careers. We did okay. And now, well now may be better than all the rest, or at least equally as good. I love my life. I can't help but smile at the thought of Georgie, my goat. If Suzanna knew I had a goat, she would certainly think I'd lost my mind. I know she thinks my age has taken me to a fairy path where imaginary happenings occur, but I feel sharper than ever, and I'm certainly sharp enough to have moved my Georgie to a friend's goat farm for a few days while she was here.

I'm thrilled to have him back. He's an old goat,

which makes me laugh, because I, too, am an old goat. We're a dandy pair.

There were moments when Suzanna and I sat together making idle talk. I held back laughter several times as I thought about what she'd think of her dignified mother wearing muck boots, hauling delivered hay to the old gardening shed off to the side of the house. Had she gone there for anything at all, she'd have found no sign of a living creature – I made sure to leave the place free of hay, free of feeding buckets, and stocked with old gardening tools. She never went to the shed though – I'm sure she thought it was filled with cobwebs and soil from years ago. It had been Henry who frequented that small but sturdy building in his efforts to grow tomatoes and peppers. He'd succeeded sometimes, other times, not so much.

Now that everything is back to normal, I suspect she'll call in a day or two to see if I'm still breathing. I suppose that's a harsh assessment of her. I do think she tries to keep an eye on her aged parent's well-being. She certainly doesn't need my money – her husband is making a fair amount with his foreign negotiations, and Suzanna herself has a successful career.

My thoughts often go to the two grandchildren who seem to care little for grandparents. I don't know if they ever visited the other set, but it was rare to see them with Henry and me. I'm not sure why it didn't bother me – perhaps because the physical distance between us kept us from getting to know one another. How does one care for a stranger, or for family who cares little to know you?

I listen to friends speak of their craving to see their grandkids, to spend time with them, and although I understand, I don't feel a pang of jealousy. My own grandparents had provided my safe place, a farm in the hills of Connecticut where I found simple peace and stability. Having been a child of an Air Force officer, we moved often. The Connecticut farm was what I thought of as home.

And I had tried to make a home for Suzanna, but she chose to leave as soon as she could. She went all the way across the country to college. I worried for her, but who was I to tell her she couldn't go? As my sister Esther would say, she was "free, white, and twenty-one." Well, eighteen, but still.

Esther had been independent too. And she was beautiful. Her hair was dark, full. Her eyes were almost violet, but my mother said they were actually brown. Esther's skin seemed paler than mine, true Irish tones. Maybe my light brown, unremarkable hair made my skin look average where Esther's looked translucent. Everyone watched Esther walk into a room – she had physical assets that drew observation, even from children. I didn't envy my sister – I wouldn't have known what to do with the attention. I studied, I read, I drew pencil sketches of trees and birds and flowers. I entertained myself with feeling complete.

Now I think of Suzanna who, like her Aunt Esther, is

extraordinarily attractive. I worried about Suzanna letting it go to her head, but it never seemed to. While I thought she was marrying young, at twenty-two, I was slightly glad to know she would be settled down. I had witnessed Esther falling victim to young Air Force men – I saw her being manipulated and often tossed aside for another. Pretty as she was, Esther's sense seemed to be slight, and I wondered if she would ever learn.

The first year that my sister, four years older than me, was married, she lost a baby at the fourth month of pregnancy. Later, many years later, I discovered through hearing my parents talking that Esther's husband had abused her – he caused the loss of their baby's life. After that, I hated him.

All of these thoughts kept me from enjoying my daughter's good looks. I was always watching the behavior of her high school dates. One wrong move and I think I might have destroyed a human being. I was quiet on the outside – ready for attack on the inside if anyone even thought to hurt my child.

That child was a girl who grew into a woman and moved across the country. Had Henry and I been such bad parents? Even when she married a Californian, I thought that someday they'd move east – we'd have a chance to repair our spirits and salvage our small family. It didn't happen, and it obviously wasn't going to.

One positive about Suzanna's departure was that I've been able to let my hair down – literally and figuratively. It was up and looking age appropriate for her approval, but I like it down. I like the natural threads of silver and white together, the below the shoulder length, and the way my hairdresser cuts the ends, making them perfectly in line with one another. I have the benefit of good hair – everyone in our family did, even my older brother. We can thank our parents for that – Dad's hair was full to his passing at eighty five, and Mother's hair was white but thick to her ninetieth year.

As I brush my silvery strands and stare into my dressing table mirror, I see the lines at and around my mouth, smaller lines at the sides of my eyes. At eighty-two, I'm not looking ancient. I think I'm what I should be – a woman who has lived a full life.

I enjoy the moisture from the ocean, working outside at my friend's farm with the goats, milking them, petting them, keeping active with physical moves that might be more than some thirty-year-olds could handle. And then there is my Georgie, who has some age and physical weaknesses – he seems to love it here with me rather than at the farm. And yet, the few days he was there during Suzanna's visit, he was fine, kept in a safe pen so that the younger, more boisterous males would leave him alone.

I can't help but laugh when I think of him in my kitchen. Suzanna would most likely be horrified to know that a farm animal was where she prepared food and sat to consume it.

How did I raise such a persnickety child?

I suppose I've always been a bit of a rebel, nothing

seemed written in stone to me. My parents must have wondered what to make of me – my brother, Douglas, followed a predictable life, and then there was Esther. I complied to some extent, but I had my own ideas from early years and managed to satisfy my unique urges. A new dress? No. A walk at my grandparents' meadows and rocky stream? Yes. Dance class for ballet precision? No. Visiting the salamanders and the cows my grandfather named? Yes. Someone was always looking for me. I'd hear my name, scramble to my feet, and meander back to what was perceived as normal. Through it all, the Air Force life, the Connecticut breaks, I found myself, or at least I built myself.

When Henry found me and decided he needed me in his life, I found him interesting, intelligent, and strong. I had my degree, but what would be next? Most of the girls my age were getting married, so why not me?

The devastation came two years after Suzanna was born while Henry and I were visiting his parents in upper state New York. I had slipped out of bed and gone downstairs toward the kitchen to have a glass of water when I overheard Henry's mother comment to her husband that she thought Henry had done okay in marrying me. I smiled to myself until I heard his father reply that he felt bad for me though because I'd never have Henry's heart. I hadn't known until then that Henry had been in love with someone else, that she'd refused him. My stomach tensed and I gave up the quest for water as I moved back upstairs to bed. I remember staring at Henry who was fast asleep, lightly snoring. I felt two emotions. First, I felt sorry for him to have known unrequited love. Second, I felt sorry for me that I'd given in and married him. My only solace was that we had Suzanna, and without Henry, she wouldn't have existed.

I lay in bed next to him that night and wondered if the girl he loved was named Suzanna. He'd chosen that name for our daughter.

Suzanna

My phone conversation with my mother was pleasant yet dry. I asked how she was – she was fine, just starting her day, she said. I thought to ask if she'd enjoyed my few days with her, but since I believed it was merely tolerable for both of us, I decided to divert the conversation to something else.

"I was thinking, the fencing around the old shed looked fairly new. Did you have that done for some reason?"

There was a noted silence on my mother's end of the line. When I said "Mother?" she answered.

"You know it was a hobby of your father's to have that little patch to grow vegetables. The old fence was falling apart, so I had a new one built."

I swallowed and remembered how he'd loved that odd little structure and growing a few tomatoes with tiny worm holes at the sides. I'd refused to eat any of what he grew. In thinking back, I might have hurt his feelings. Maybe I hadn't been the best daughter in the universe.

I did have a momentary thought that my mother's

reasoning was pretty sketchy – building a fence in memory of my father's small garden? I supposed I needed to expect these things – certainly at her age a measure of mysteriousness might occasionally appear. I would need to keep in close contact with her, just in case. Then again, what else did she have to do with her time other than find things around the house and her yard to fix up. Not five minutes after hanging up with my mother, Glenn finally called, I was so glad to hear his voice that I didn't question why he hadn't checked in the evening before. He gave no reasoning for the time of his call and I let it go. It crossed my mind that he might have met someone there, that after thirty years of marriage, maybe he was attracted to someone new. I rushed those thoughts away – there was little I could do to verify his every moment or what he was thinking. I decided not to mention anything that could lead to an argument and no resolve.

Unfortunately, the two conversations meant that I was running behind schedule. I took a quick shower and dressed for work then decided to have coffee there rather than make my own.

Before leaving, I go through my usual routine of looking around at the house – making sure nothing is plugged in that shouldn't be, nothing is out of place, all doors are locked. It's a textbook copy of a Frank Lloyd Wright design – beautiful, placid, and empty.

Maybe I need a dog. My parents always had animals – dogs and cats. Glenn had been reluctant to have a pet –

he teased that he had me.

* * *

After eleven hours of meetings, programs for new trainees, and paperwork that never seemed up to date, I start home stopping only to pick up a sandwich for my dinner. Lunch had been two cups of black coffee and a cookie at my desk.

Dusk settles in as I pull onto my gravel driveway. We'd chosen the material to add to the natural look of the redwood and stone house, but I like the sound of the tires crunching the durable stone, awakening my spirit to relaxation and aloneness.

I turn the engine off, but my hand doesn't reach for the door handle. I question myself: Do I prefer the alone times to the forced conversations I've been having with Glenn, with the kids, with my mother? Is everything I do out of duty rather than genuine caring? Or is it a combination of emptiness we've learned from one another?

I shake my head. There's no answer to those questions. Who can tell?

Stepping from the car to the path which leads to the front door, I sort through my keyring to find the house key and unlock the door before stepping inside. The lights we always left on were dim and soothing – enough to see by. I love the house, the openness, the huge windows overlooking the woods, the occasional deer meandering around the property. Everything is so perfect. Except for me. I am outrageously lonely.

As I eat my sandwich and sip some coffee, I ponder the reasons for my emptiness. The few friends we'd known from college as newlyweds had moved on. We hadn't bothered to accumulate friends after marriage; Glenn was working on his doctorate, and I was taking care of the kids. At the time, the wonderful house and the four of us were enough. We were operating independently and seemingly well. After all, my parents had only one another, and that had always sufficed.

I put my plate and mug into the sink and drift into the living room to sit in Glenn's recliner. Despite it being completely dark outside, I don't turn on more lights. Maybe in the darkness I can hide from all I'm feeling. I switch on the TV then press the mute button. I watch the colorful screen for a few moments then close my eyes.

I understand that I'm fortunate to own a home, a nice home, to have a good job, and to have a family. But then I question how well I'd done with that family – the cohesive qualities seemed to be missing. My son and daughter had no interest in one another, and they were in opposite areas of the country. My husband was often in Japan while I kept the home fires burning.

I laugh aloud, mocking my thought – I open my eyes and stare at the massive fireplace which has never been used. Glenn claimed fires were smoky and probably not good for any of us to breathe. I know better though. I love a blazing fire – my parents always had them in Boston as well as at the beach house on the Cape.

My eyes rise to the painting over the mantle. Upscale

modern art, shades of blue and orange – vibrant, thought-provoking, but with no suggestion of a title. To me it looked like the raging ocean, and maybe the orange was a warm island or a volcano. I wasn't sure. Maybe it was representative of my life, an isolation surrounded by impossible passage.

My thoughts travel back to my mother. It's near midnight on her side of the country. I picture her in bed, asleep. I turn the TV sound up and listen to the noise.

Sadearah

I fed Georgie and swept out his shed. I think he hoped for an evening in my kitchen. He must remember getting corn muffins and cranberry scones there. Not that I don't enjoy his company, but he isn't at all neat and tonight I was up for a quiet cup of tea and a salad with blue cheese. Now, at nearly the witching hour, I just want to sit and let Ravel lull me to sleep. Sometimes I need music without lyrics, nothing to make me think more than I already do. Although, stretched out in bed, my mind often goes where it wishes even when I demand that it return.

Not that I worry about my only child, but I often wonder how Suzanna is enjoying her life. I used to wonder that about my own mother. My father had his Air Force career, and he liked reading about the Civil War – he could discuss it with the best. My mother seemed vaguely lost, as though nothing was of particular interest. She lived in starched dresses, shoes with two inch heels, stockings even in the hottest of summers. I wondered what could possibly be going on in her head.

Nothing was evident.

It was her parents who owned the farm in Connecticut, and I could not figure out how she ever left there. To me, the place was Heaven, and, of course, it's gone now with my grandparents, but my mother grew up with sixty-plus acres of glorious meadows and Berkshire Hills – nothing and no one would have taken me from that.

What was it that seemed so great about traipsing around the world with a fellow she'd only met six months earlier? My father was a nice man, a smart man, and he was kind to my brother, sister, and me. He was considerate of our mother, always complimented her on the evening meal. But then he went to his chair and read, leaving Mother to tidy the kitchen, Esther and me at her elbows, before she retired to a sewing basket where she mended socks and sewed on missing buttons.

One evening when Esther was out, my brother, Douglas was at a night college, and Dad was in bed, my mother talked to me about her concerns for my sister. I thought Esther, at nineteen, was in complete control of her wishes ready to spread her wings. I was fifteen – what did I know? My mother grew angry at my suggestion that she should just stop worrying about Esther. I argued that my sister had always done what she wanted and probably wouldn't change. With those words spoken, my mother's face grew tight and she said something terrible to me. She asked what I knew at my age and called me a name I have never revealed. The name was a common part of all lives, and I knew it would stay with me for life. I'm eighty-two, so yes, for sixty-seven years I've thought every single day about what she called me. It shattered my spirit that night because I knew then that no matter what she claimed, she didn't love her third child. I wondered many times if she had said something as hurtful to Douglas or Esther.

My mother obviously had her collection of discontent, and I wondered after that evening if she had regretted giving into the plea from my father to become a military wife. I thought, too, of the damage a parent can do with the wrong words to their child. After years of brief thoughts on the subject, often late at night when my world was quiet, I would tell myself that parents were just people, and people make mistakes. We revere parents, thinking of them as protectors, guides to a safe and happy life. It isn't always so.

Every now and then I think of how Henry and I raised Suzanna. Henry insisted she attend a private school in Boston which seemed to fit her well. We both had an interest in art and music which exposed our child at an early age to love the symphony and The Museum of Fine Art. We took her to children's events and invited her friends to join us – we were conscious of having an only child and didn't want her to be lonely. What then did we do to make her choose a college on the West Coast and then to stay there?

Henry was quiet about losing his beautiful daughter to Glenn and to California, and I felt forlorn, wondering how we had failed.

I don't feel old in spite of my eighty-two years. If I were even ten years younger, I'd do as my friends and have a little goat farm, but I wouldn't sell the males. That's how I came to take Georgie – he was about to be sold. At nearly sixteen, and a life span of maybe twenty years, I thought it was grossly unfair for him to be taken for someone's kids to ride on or, worse, to become a parcel of meals. He and I have been friends for almost a year now. My hope is to have him around for at least another three, maybe four years. I just needed to hide him at the farm when Suzanna was coming here – she would definitely reject my having a farm animal. She grew up with umpteen million cats and several dogs over the years but to my knowledge had just one cat who died many years ago. I will never understand how I raised such a woman, one who seems not to think much for her deceased father and very alive mother and who has not at this time even a bird in a cage. She mystifies me. Perhaps we're a failure as family. I don't know, and it's too late to start anew.

Mentally I make my next day list. I will get up in the morning to a sweet August day, make coffee, get dressed, then head to Georgie's shed. He will be fed, given fresh water in his trough, and allowed out to roam around in the paddock. He has a nice area – always in shade from a few generous pines which sometimes he eats. I will treat him with a carrot and an apple. His eyes will thank me.

All this commiserating with myself makes me smile at nearly one in the morning. I should go to bed. I should stop thinking. I should close my eyes and use mindfulness to lull myself into wonderland. I'll try.

After a last sip of tea I rinse my cup and shut off the bright kitchen light. A small lantern with not more than a glow is left on as I turn to my bedroom for rest. On my bed, on my back staring at the darkened ceiling, I try to think of the rolling waves, the endless ebb of the tides, the supple seagrass swaying in the wind with beach plum growing nearby. Every day is an enlightenment – living by the insistent water which stretches itself to the shores of Europe. I cannot help but wonder what secrets it knows, this vast ocean traveling to and fro.

Was it wrong of me to stay distant from my daughter? I question that with genuine concern. My sister and brother have passed on. I have no other family alive but Suzanna, her Glenn, and the children who are no longer children. What, I question myself for about the thousandth time, caused this break in our once companionable unit? I wanted to figure it out, but with what for assistance? I close my eyes to the shaded ceiling and think again about the sand and the surf. I need rest or I'll be napping in tomorrow's afternoon when I could be reading or sitting with my eyes to the ocean. The closer I've grown to this age, the more I hope to accomplish. Tomorrow I will make waffles, and I will share them with Georgie. There, with that nice thought I will sleep.

Suzanna

It's Saturday and Glenn isn't home from his trip. I used to look forward to the weekends when we'd head to Milgate Park for summer concerts with a picnic in tow and a good bottle of wine. It's been at least three years since he and I did any such thing. I wish for more than I have, not in property, not in possessions, but in simply having a memorable, companionable life.

He was vague on the phone about when he'd be back, the negotiations often involving going to a client's home for an overnight, dinners arranged with associates. Glenn has always made it seem like a task, packing and leaving for distant shores. Will there be any end to this? Am I stuck in this life with a good job, a great house, and that's it?

My thoughts drift easily to the times I had as a child in Boston, skating on Frog Pond in the Common, seeing ballet, museums, and heading to the North End for good Italian food. My parents introduced me to a world beyond their living room. I'm grateful for what they offered, and at the same time I question what made me

26

move away. I often thought that they were a pair with little room for a third being, but as I've matured, I've realized that I wouldn't have known what to do any better than they. I was offered a lively assortment of activities, and I had friends, yet here I am, alone on the other side of the country. Why did we fall into this awkward space where communication seems hard? Do we even like one another, my mother and me?

I think about Annette, once my best friend back in Boston. She lived near us and attended my school. We were inseparable for years, each of us enthusiastic stamp collectors, savoring the colorful designs and storing them in leather journals.

When I went to college, she and I stayed close through letters and phone calls, but she attended Boston University and found other friends who took my place. I was upset, felt disappointed in her decision to be unavailable to me when I went home for visits, but she seemed aloof, almost angry that I had abandoned her. That had never been my intent. And while she didn't speak the words, it seemed evident to me that she no longer, or maybe never, cared for me. It made me all the more determined to stay away from the east – I needed to find my own life without these people.

Thinking of Annette, my thoughts return to my mother. I left *her*, she didn't leave me. Yet what provided the urge to go away? I wonder now if I felt I had no place there, that my parents were sufficient with just the two of them, that maybe I was the cross they had to carry.

Sitting back in my chair, I stare at the ceiling and feel empty. Yes, I have a husband and children. Yes, I have a beautiful home. Yes, I have an important, and for the most part, fulfilling job. Still, something's missing.

My meanderings from window to window provide me with views of the redwoods and beautiful greens which seem to be a sort of fern. My parents would know exactly what they were called, but I never paid much attention to names of things unfamiliar to me. I suppose that's not the best way to manage life, being a subtle observer.

I'm not going to allow additional thoughts of Annette into my head. She is part of the past, her choice. No sense in dwelling on what is lost or damaged. What I will do is keep a tighter rein on my mother. Surely I should be watching for physical and mental declines – she's eighty-two and all alone out there on the beach, not where anyone would see her if she fell. She could be days trapped in her own place, or even outside. And who would know?

Sadearah

It's Saturday noon. I've fed Georgie and let him outside – he's a sweet creature, and I swear those big eyes see me more perfectly than any human I ever knew.

With coffee in hand I'll enjoy the ocean view from my Adirondack chair – maybe I'll sit in the one Suzanna always chooses, maybe I'll gain a better understanding of what she's all about. I wonder what she and her husband are doing today. They're hours behind me, but still, they must be having breakfast together or something as pleasant. It would have been nice these past thirty plus years if we'd been closer, geographically as well as emotionally. Some things aren't in the cards I suppose.

When I think back to the years Henry and I had together, in spite of a few glitches, we generally had a good life. We were considerate of one another. When I was sick, he brought me soup and an extra blanket. When he was sick, I did the same. We compromised on what to do when we had a day to simply enjoy – I often was ready for a drive north toward or to New

29

Hampshire. He would sometimes suggest something closer, another Cape destination for lunch. We did some of each. Now I'm left to make all decisions, and I'm sure Suzanna would scold me for some of my escapades. I simply don't confide in her when I decide to drive north or to spend a day driving three hours to the Connecticut farm I so loved. My driving skills are fine – if I get tired, I stop for coffee, which is how I met Stephen in Connecticut nearly a year ago. Although he's more my daughter's age than mine, we had a nice conversation over coffee and decided to keep in touch. I have zero interest in a physical relationship with anyone, even if his name was God. But I do like the easy flow of topics Stephen and I come up with. He's an interesting man. However, I don't need to tell Suzanna about him yet, if ever.

I think often of my grandmother – not a simple woman, she had a great sense of humor and skills in the kitchen. I marveled at the complicated home she made appear like pictures from a good magazine. Her personality was easy, and you could ask her anything and there was always a credible answer. I missed all of that. Maybe I'd head back there soon, and I could let Stephen know so that perhaps we could have coffee together again.

I miss my Henry. I'm so sorry he's gone. Yet I've found ways to find detailed pleasure in most days. I miss my dogs and cats, but at my age, I think it's fair for me to take only older animals, like Georgie. If something happened to me, they'd take him back at the goat farm, and he wouldn't be pampered, but he'd at least be someplace familiar. I hope every night when I climb into my bed that I will be there for him in the morning. I've had friends who went to bed and died, no warning, so I know it's possible. My wish to live another clump of years may not happen. We have no control over our destiny. I accept that.

There are times, too, when I wish I knew if that girl Henry loved was named Suzanna. That would certainly irk me. Maybe it's best I don't know, besides there's no way to discover that fact. Everyone who knew Henry is gone. What would I do anyway? Change Suzanna's name to something I liked such as Sarah? Too late. I need to stop reminiscing about the past. Henry and I had a good forty-seven years together. We were kind to one another. It was a partnership that worked.

There haven't been many women I haven't gotten along with. Even my sister, Esther, who I did not want to be anything like, I found interesting and easy to love. I wanted her to wise up, to stop taking flattery and flirtations so seriously – too many men, and many she knew wanted her for the night or for a few months. She fell for it every time, and even at the age of thirteen I was more suspecting than she was at seventeen. She made me worry.

Years spent in the Boston area were busy working for a textbook company editing and raising a child. I had two good friends, Ruthie Davis and Amelia Brand.

Before I moved here to the Cape, both of them were gone. Ruthie died in her seventies in her own bed – we were all shocked. Amelia ended up in a terrible nursing home where I visited her for months before she passed on. I didn't expect to meet new friends here on the Cape, but I wandered into the little store for goat cheese and met the McMann family, which is where I help out and how I ended up with Georgie Boy. Everything is pretty much okay. Some might think I'd be lonely living on this shoreline by myself, no close neighbors, just me and a goat. But I'm good.

Haven't heard from Suzanna. Maybe I should give her a call later today, maybe this evening, although maybe they're off to an opera or something. I can envision her dark brown hair, like her father's, against a black lace dress to her ankles. Suzanna used to love dressing up, and I'd bet that hasn't changed. My own days of going to the symphony or a play with Henry are over. I enjoyed them, but I've had enough of that and this life suits me well. How grateful I am to be able to sit with coffee and my feet up each morning after caring for Georgie, and then poking around or reading to suit my mood. Yes, I'll definitely head to Connecticut soon and I'll give Stephen a call to see if we could meet for an hour over coffee and a sandwich.

Maybe old folks like me have too much time to think. I don't believe that's true though. I get up each day with determination – chores and then whatever in heck I want. I love remembering those who crossed my path, family or friends, and the last thing I'd want is to forget they existed. I miss some of them terribly, and sometimes I lose a tear or two, especially over my dear pets, but I would rather have sad moments than not recall them. And then I think about what's around the next corner. Every second of every day has unexpected happenings, like me meeting Stephen, and like finding and adopting Georgie. Change is good, it allows one to grow, to be amazed – it's a wonderful gift.

There are fewer times I think back to my mother. She was an attractive woman, but I don't remember seeing her laugh or even smile much. In fact I can't remember that at all. She was always busy, washing windows, polishing the furniture, sweeping the tile in her military kitchens, vacuuming the carpets. My heavens, did she ever have any fun? Her life, to me, seemed self-imprisoning. She hated it when my brother left home for school and then a career, living on his own. She seemed worried about Esther, and I didn't wonder why. And with me, I felt like the extra child who wasn't expected or wanted. She tolerated me, I think expecting me to fail at something. But I didn't. I had my education, I loved to read, and when I married, I married well.

I think of the name she called me when she was angry with me for sticking up for Esther – that name, that terrible utterance from her lips was unkind. No, it was appalling – how did a parent say something like that to their child? I'd never speak that way to Suzanna.

But I'm sure I failed her in other ways. She didn't

33

have her grandparents around much. My parents stayed in the Air Force beyond years expected and were never close by. Henry's parents were in Upstate New York and never once traveled to Boston where we worked and lived. We went to them a few times, but they were not exactly welcoming and warm. I didn't beg to go there, and Henry didn't seem to miss the family who'd raised him. It's really quite a wonder that anyone survives with sanity when so many personalities invade our lives and sometimes cause havoc.

I can't help but smile when I think of what I've experienced and how I've managed to find the energy to laugh and deal with problems I thought might not be so easy to solve. But they *were* solved, even Henry's sudden death, shocking as it was, sent every cell in my body working on how to best adjust. I had no regrets in parting with the house Henry insisted on living in, and I had no problem moving here to the shore. It's my most perfect place. Everything here has what I need. Memories flow as I recall Henry collecting beach plums in an old tin bucket, and me wandering around barefoot, enjoying the silky sand beneath my feet. Even Suzanna used to love coming here, and then she disappeared out west and that was the end of that.

I'll call her later. Why shouldn't I? She calls me every now and then. We're amicable, and if I call her once in a while, it will certainly let her know that I haven't faded away and forgotten that I have a child.

Goodness, eighty-two is a marvelous age.

Suzanna

I cannot believe that my mother just called me, and in the middle of my concerns about Glenn.

He sounded vague on the phone, as though he might be tired or maybe avoiding conversation. Sometimes I don't know what to make of him. He's a brilliant man, but that's not enough for me anymore. Maybe it never was. He dazzled me in college, and he's certainly been a very good provider yet something's missing. When he comes home, I'll talk to him about our lives. After thirty years and no more expensive colleges to pay for, aren't we entitled to slow our pace and enjoy ourselves?

And my mother, what was the purpose of her call? She never calls me. Did she forget that? I suppose I'll have to worry about that now, that she's making changes due to her age.

I recall sitting with her in those old Adirondacks Dad bought. I tried not to be obvious as I looked at her face. She has more wrinkles than anyone I've ever seen, or noticed. Too much time in the sun I expect. Her eyes are bright though, and her eyelashes enviable. Her eyebrows as well, all silvery white. She and I look nothing alike – I'm a carbon copy of Dad. But my mother, she's really exquisite looking in spite of her years. No wonder Dad fell for her, and besides having great features, she was calm, placid in her efforts to raise me. Maybe that's why she annoys me so much –no matter what I did she never lost her cool. I tried, I wanted her to show some emotion, but it was Dad's stern looks in my direction that stopped me from going too far. I wonder, did Mother simply not know what to do with me?

Kira was too much like me. She gave her bewildered parents a run for our money. I remember thinking that I didn't deserve such an independent and difficult daughter, but maybe I did. I don't know. It's not easy raising kids. I had no idea at all that Jordan was gay. He dated girls in high school and in college. At least I thought he was. I have no idea what he was doing because he went to college in Arizona. His music led him to New Mexico and then to Michael. That was a shocker, at least to me. Glenn didn't seem that surprised.

Sometimes I feel a little melancholy about Kira. She's moved so far away, three thousand miles to New York City. I suppose I did the same when I opted for an education and life here. I could have had even a day with her when I visited Mother. It would have been easy to hop a train or something to New York, but she said she didn't have time. Really? She had no time at all to see her mother? Maybe it's payback.

I remember Kira's best friend in grammar school and

then high school, Jennifer Holmes. I used to think that Kira would be more appreciative for the life we gave her knowing that Jennifer was living in fear from one day to the other. Her mother was taken to the hospital, bruised and bleeding, the father, an attorney, having nearly killed the woman. I could not understand how Margaret Holmes put up with that terrible man. What if he had begun to hurt the children? Poor Jennifer. She loved coming here to stay a weekend now and then, and no wonder.

I suppose I shouldn't be so picky about the time Glenn spends in Japan. He's never laid a hand on me or the kids – that matters. Not that I'd have put up with either. I was raised to know my worth.

My father was such an intellectual person, always reading books one might study in college. He was smart, but I wonder what kind of marriage my parents actually had. Now he's gone, eight long years, and Mother is puttering around on a beach. What in hell does she do with herself day after day? She doesn't even have a cat anymore. She told me she's too old to get a cat, she could find herself incapacitated or dead, and then what would happen to the cat? She worries about things like that.

I think I'll need to visit her more often, just to keep an eye on her adjusted living. Old age is frightening. The body weakens and the spirit begins to fade away. I wonder if she just sits out in those uncomfortable chairs all day, the sun beaming down on that straw hat of hers, drying her skin until it will finally be like old leather. It's horrible. I dread getting older.

I think I'll follow my mother's example and call my kids tonight, both of them. I rarely hear from my handsome Jordan, so talented. And Kira doesn't call all that often either. I understand that she's busy, but a five-minute phone call isn't a possibility? Every time she calls she prefaces her comments with telling me she's only got a minute, she's on her way out for dinner with friends, out to a show, out. Does she not realize how limiting that is to our relationship? I suppose I don't hold much interest for a young woman of twenty-six. She's made a place for herself in the world and I guess I should be glad of that. I am glad, somewhat.

Is this what I gave to my own parents? Maybe I taught Kira how to behave. I was barely eighteen coming here, California dreamin'. Then there was Glenn, and then no more East Coast. It must have seemed strange to my parents, an only child who just flew the coop.

I liked the feeling of being independent of them – after college, going back to live at home was not in my plans. Jordan and Kira did the same and I hated it. I wonder if my parents hated what I did. They never said so. They did try to persuade me to wait a year or two to marry.

Maybe I'll visit Mother again in the spring or early summer, and then I'll just pop in on Kira without asking. I'd really like to see her, to be closer to her. And Jordan,

I'd so love to spend some time with him, but this thing he has going with Michael is awkward. I don't think I'd know how to deal with that situation. Staying with them, that just wouldn't work.

Good Lord, maybe everything I've done all my life has been slightly tilted. Maybe I need a good confidant, a friend, someone I could talk with. Everything feels disconnected. All I have to take care of now is that big old rubber tree plant.

Mother's phone call was so weird. I still can't figure out what she called for. She said something about giving me a ring to see how I was. She's never done that before. She asked about Glenn and the kids. I didn't tell her that Jordan is gay, and I didn't tell her that Kira was too busy to see me when I was east. I didn't tell her much of anything. God, she really may be sinking. All that beauty, that stamina she showed when Dad passed suddenly. What is she made of? I don't know what I'd do if Glenn died. I think I'd just sit in his recliner until I shriveled up and died myself. I breathe in and out. I have no life. Even though he's alive, he's hardly here. Maybe my life wouldn't be so different after all.

How *would* I feel if Glenn died? Just thinking about it seems impossible – he's filled with energy for his work and he's passionate about this house and land. How could Glenn die? He couldn't leave all this.

And yet I wonder how he feels about me. We've been together for more than thirty years. Would he miss *me*? Obviously he does fine without me while away in Japan.

I need to stop saturating myself in reflective thinking. I have an empty garden that I could buy plants for. I could rearrange the study book shelves, and they're certainly in need of a good dusting. Maybe I could get rid of some of the old textbooks we've saved over the years. Between work and this house, I could keep busier and there wouldn't be so much time to think.

And I will call my mother more often. I have the feeling she's going to be a bit of a problem – something's up with her calling me. That was just plain strange. When I go east again, maybe I'll look around at places that might be appropriate for her when she becomes irrational. That's exactly what I need to do – I'll check out a few good nursing homes.

Sadearah

Talking with Suzanna is like a combination of speaking with a dictator and a cat. I'm not clear about why I bother. She seemed both surprised and irritated that I called her. She calls me, but it seems that's all fine in her mind – she probably thinks I'm not doing anything. Where, she must wonder, did I find the nerve to call *her*? When Henry was alive I left it to him. He'd pick up the phone every now and then to call her, demanding in his fatherly way to know how she and her family were doing. Good for Henry, not so good for me. Oh well, I won't do that again – I didn't enjoy a solitary second of my connection to my own blood and guts.

Looking out the window, I see Georgie and he makes me smile. I miss my former fur family of dogs and cats. I need an old timer like my handsome goat. And while the shelter had no older ones when I checked last year, I should check again. What's Suzanna going to do about that? She has no business or control over what I do, and anyway, why would she think to care? Good for me – I'm getting feisty in my old age.

I remember when Cindy and Natalie, once good friends of mine, hated one another. Cindy told me that Natalie had a bad odor emitting from her body. I'd known that, kind of a musty essence. It didn't bother me. I knew it was something she couldn't control and that it wasn't because she was dirty.

Natalie hated Cindy because Cindy always had to be right, no matter what the subject. When I introduced them, I thought they'd get along fine. Each one was an avid sewing enthusiast, so I expected them to share that interest. That did not happen. They disliked one another and each complained to me for more than a year which made me uneasy.

Then came the day when Cindy invited Natalie to her home for lunch. She later told me about it and I was perplexed. How did that happen? Why just the two of them? Natalie never mentioned it to me, nor I to her. But Cindy wanted me to know that she had befriended Natalie and asked if that bothered me, the two of them having lunch together, without me. I was stunned for something to say and ultimately said I didn't mind. After we'd hung up though, the more I thought about it, the more it did bother me, but I decided to let it go. And I wondered why Cindy told me.

A few weeks later Cindy called to tell me she and Natalie had gone out for an ice cream cone. She asked if I minded that they didn't invite me. I said no. They knew I couldn't eat too much ice cream since milk products tended to bother my stomach, but I might have gone and had a cup of coffee. That nonsense went on for a couple of years as I recall.

The end of them came when Natalie needed surgery that was a bit precarious. I knew she had very little in family and said I would go to the hospital with her the morning she needed to check in. The night before, too late to reverse the decision with Natalie, Cindy called to tell me that Natalie didn't want me to go with her. That did it for me. I let go of both of them after Natalie recovered. I never said why. I ignored their phone calls and they eventually stopped calling.

I will never understand how people can be so mean-spirited, but I don't miss them. I have no idea to this day, nearly twenty years later, how they are or if they are still chums. And I don't care. What I care about is that I survived whatever it was that Cindy wanted to burden me with. It makes me wonder though how an old friend like Natalie allowed it to happen.

Life as I see it is a varied mix. Some things work out, others don't. I don't take it personally because that hurts. I don't hate Cindy and Natalie, but I'll do my best to not cross their paths again.

The problem for me at this stage of my life is that while I have a circle of friends, nice people, a couple of them are not well and another couple moved to a warmer climate. I like it right here at the shores with my feet in the sand, my nose sniffing salt air, and my life being private. We're born by ourselves, no matter how much intervention, and we die the same way. I am thrilled to be an individual and in sole control of how I proceed. That's why I don't bother to tell Suzanna much of anything about my life. She's on the other side of the country, so what does she care? It's none of her business anyway.

Suzanna would probably be shocked if she knew I associated with a few women her age. One lives down the beach from me. Kate and I met a few years ago while walking the shore looking for sea glass and shells. She invited me for tea, I invited her for lemonade. Her heart had been broken by her husband's betrayal, mine by Henry's death. We had a link and still enjoy an hour together every now and then. She laughs at Georgie, and she always has a treat for him when she comes to visit us.

Yes, I do believe that this is the time of my life. Some would disagree, declaring that age is against me. Age has nothing to do with anything. I've known people like my brother and sister who died too young, as misfortunes came their way. I've known children who died, babies who never drew a breath, and I am supposed to care that at eighty-two I am closer to the end? So what? Who of us knows, at any age, how close or far we are from our graves? Henry didn't want to die, and that saddened me because he seemed frightened. Yet I, who intensely dislike the dark, am not afraid. When I close my eyes at night, even with low light in my bedroom, I am in the dark. I expect the same when I breathe my last. Meanwhile, I have the life I want, and how many walking this earth can say that?

Every once in a while I emotionally punch myself with the question about who, if any, loved me. I wish I thought Henry did, that would give me some comfort, but having heard his parents' conversation about a former love, I've wondered too many years about being second best. I know he cared for me. He was always tender and kind, but there's a difference between being cared about and being loved. And I have no recollection of being loved in my birth family – I made it uneven being the third child. I didn't fit in. My father was kind but too busy to pay any attention to his quiet one, and my mother was a complex story in herself. That name she called me still sticks to my skin. Then again, I'm not sure she loved anyone. Maybe some people can't – they don't know how. So, here I am, knowing how to love too well and feeling a little left out. There's no one here to love – no child, no grandchildren, no true-heart friends…just my pets. However, I'll never shed a tear about that issue. I'm alive and well and happy as a clam, although I never understood how anyone could possibly know how happy a clam is.

Tomorrow morning I'll go to the goat farm and help out. I've got to remember to get some cheese while I'm there, and I'll be able to enjoy seeing the three new babies. When I get back home, I'll give Georgie a few grapes and a handful of kale then I'll put my feet in the sand while I sit with lemonade and stare at the rolling waves. I may even take my journal out there with me and write a few lines, maybe take liberty with a poem or two.

I wonder sometimes about all I have accrued, what Suzanna will do with my stuff when I'm gone. No doubt, she'll toss much of it away, not knowing or caring that I have valuable pieces in gold, that I have sentimental items from childhood and a pretty rock from my grandparents' Connecticut farm. Treasures will be discarded one way or another. I suppose that's why I like antiques. They are other souls' cherished hoards being loved once again.

I do have the life.

Suzanna

I wish Glenn would come home. I know these foreign dealings take negotiating and that he has no choice other than to stay until there's a conclusion, but I'm not particularly good at alone times. I seem to have a lot of them. Especially lately.

I keep thinking about my mother's call a few days ago. She has me confused. It's never been like her to pick up the phone. She was the one who sent the cards and checks for birthdays, holidays, anniversaries. It was my father who called to see how we were. I miss that relationship, that union.

Work keeps me busy, but what fills me up? Certainly not my kids who have chosen to live a distance away. My husband spends a lot of time in Japan, so he doesn't add to my joy. We have no pets, no friends. Maybe I'm self-isolated. I have, after all, made this happen. Haven't I? Shouldn't I have expected that if I left people behind they'd fill in with others and forget about me? I thought I had enough with Glenn and the kids, but they're gone, at least the kids are gone, and I can't imagine them ever returning. And Glenn, he's away so much. What am I

47

doing living out here in the woods on my own?

Maybe I should join a social group or committee of some sort. I know there are environmentalists in town, and they're always looking for help. I like anything to do with preserving the trees, the lakes, Earth in general. Maybe that's what I need, an interest and new people to associate with. I haven't ever done anything without Glenn, but it's likely time. He's only in his fifties, so I can't imagine he'll retire any time soon. That means I will face more of this, years without companionship. I'll have to see what I can find on the internet about the committee – when they meet, what they do, maybe even who else is involved. It's sad, but part of the reason I haven't ever had too many friends is probably because I don't think much of most other people. There are few who I find interesting, who I sincerely want to engage with. People can cause pain, can disappoint, can leave you alone.

So here I sit with the phone one foot away. It's after seven at night. I should be having dinner with Glenn, or someone, and I'm by myself. Tomorrow I'll change some of that by getting involved in a worthwhile endeavor, making this planet healthier.

God, I'm thinking like my mother.

And then I'll call my kids. I mean, what am I afraid of? Rejection, I suppose, and that's because they don't come here very often and they don't invite us to visit where they live. That's a kick in the head. I wonder if that's what caused my mother to call me. Maybe she wanted to reach out. And I was short with her because her timing didn't suit me. I should call her, apologize. Maybe in a few days.

It's definitely important to make a change, or else I'll go completely crazy. Great house, great job, and nothing. Who will make the change if it's not me?

I miss feeling unified with my own husband and kids. It was so much easier when Glenn wasn't traveling constantly for the firm and when the kids were little in size and resistance. Maybe I'm a control freak. It was just easier. While I'm glad that Jordan and Kira seem happy in their lives, the whole situation leaves me feeling empty. I need a refill, and it's up to me to make that happen.

Maybe that's what my mother did after Dad died. She's there alone and yet she doesn't seem exactly sad about that. Though I guess I don't know much about her life. I'll give her a call in a few days...not that we have much to say. We're like aliens who are unfamiliar with one another's planets. Maybe I'll mention that I'm thinking of getting a pet – see if she has any suggestions.

I'm tired of being an island; it's time for me to connect, to form a bridge to people of a like mind.

I feel better already. I have a plan. Get involved in something that interests me. Call my kids and my mother in the evening to check in with them. Make more of a life for me. And maybe for some animal too.

Sadearah

Suzanna is confusing me with her more than average number of calls. I wonder if she thinks I need to be checked on frequently since I'm living alone. Except for Georgie, of course, my well-kept secret, but I guess he wouldn't be too much help in an emergency.

I know she questions my memory. She wasn't very subtle about that when she was last here. I forget every now and then where I put things, like postage stamps that Henry once kept in his bedroom desk. And the bird seed, sometimes after I fill the feeders I plop the sack of seed down wherever I am. I suppose I could be better at placing things like that in more conspicuous places, but eventually I find them. It's just a little embarrassing when Suzanna is watching me like I'm a swirling dervish. I'll have to keep that in mind when she's here again – I'll be more on my toes. God sakes, I dread her next visit.

What happened to the dreams I had for her when she was tiny and seemed to like me? We had those days when we baked cookies, cupcakes, made mouse burgers for Henry. I can't help but laugh when I think of those burgers, formed with ground beef into a mouse face. The first time she excitedly told Henry we had mouse burgers for him, his expression was one of horror. I truly believe he first thought we had used mice to create part of his dinner.

Oh well, I'll figure things out before she comes again. I should be able to enjoy my own child, but she's too ready to pounce on me these days. I find it sad.

When I go back a little further, I remember how I felt when I was with my mother. She taught Esther how to cook, how to make a cake, how to frost it, the sides first then the top. I watched from afar, having been told to stay back. Stay back? Why? In the end, I took care of my mother since Esther seemed in turmoil over a failing marriage. I cared that my mother was comfortable, but I didn't love her. I feel a little ashamed of that, but then again, I know she didn't want me, she didn't love me. I believe she loved Doug, but I wasn't sure how she felt about Esther. I was sure about me.

While it's on my mind, I'll go fill the bird feeders and then maybe have a sit in my Adirondack. Those slanted seats aren't the easiest things to get out of, but I do like the way they tilt back and make me feel securely planted. Now, where did I leave the seed this time?

Ah ha. There it is. I'm glad that the weather is still to the point where I don't need a sweater – at least I don't today. Just one more thing to love about New England.

I pass through the back door and move from one

feeder to the next. Now that the two feeders are filled, the chickadees will be grateful. I'll just leave the seed sack here by Henry's chair, and I'll take it inside later.

Oh, the arm of his chair is showing decay. This is not good. It looks unsafe. The constant sea mist and blazing sun are causing the old wood to decompose. I wonder how bad it is. Now I've done it. I pressed too hard and the arm is half off and I can see that one of the slats on the seat is cracked. Henry's chair is broken, probably beyond repair. If he was here, he'd mend it with new wood, but there's just me. I should have put these chairs away when out of season, but I can't shove them in the shed where Georgie might injure himself – there's not adequate room for summer furniture and a fairly large goat.

Before Suzanna comes again I'll buy new chairs, maybe something better than these old Adirondacks. They're at least forty years old. She won't be here again now for a long while, at least I don't believe she will. Maybe I'll look at teak – that's more weather resilient. And I'll find a pair of chairs, or maybe even a nice bench, something easier to get up from. I'm no spring chicken anymore – the knees are not always happy with the positions I get into, and that's all I need, Suzanna picking on me as she watches me struggle with getting upright. Am I supposed to feel ashamed for aging? Well, I don't.

That's it, new chairs or a nice bench with a back and arms. Maybe I can find something on my next little journey to Connecticut. That will need to be soon. I miss the old farm. Maybe I'll give Stephen a call and see if he'd have time to meet for lunch. He's such a nice fellow. I love a pleasant conversation where I can relax and not feel judged. I find it dismal that my own daughter seems to think so poorly of me. I can't fix it. Obviously her mind has been made up.

When Henry was here it seemed they had an attachment that had bypassed me. She liked him best, that was evident. It felt awful to me for years, but once I grew used to being shunned and often made fun of, I worked at ignoring the entire situation. I wondered at times what it would have been like if we'd had a son as well. Might a son have loved me as his mom? I suppose that's where Stephen comes in. I bet he has a good relationship with his mother.

Sitting here next to a disintegrated seat makes me wonder if my own chair is also on its way to a wood pile. It seems sturdy enough. I'll sit here for now, but maybe I shouldn't wait for a trip to Connecticut to find replacements. Tomorrow I'll check into new chairs in town. I know Mr. Roberts will deliver whatever I buy. What was I thinking about buying furniture in Connecticut? However would I get it from the car? I'm glad Suzanna wasn't here to listen in on my thoughts. She'd really worry about me then.

It's strange how Henry's seat fell apart. Of course he was a big man, nearly a foot taller than I am, and heavier as well. He loved his morning coffee in these chairs when we came for the summers. I wonder what he'd think if he knew I sold the big house and moved here. He never would have consented to life at the beach, but here I am, pleased with this simple existence.

It was all lovely going to the theater and symphony, but how much of that was I to continue with when I'd be making the arrangements and going alone? I like what I have, the uncomplicated measure of each day and the memories.

I miss so much of what once surrounded me, and yet I've managed to adjust. You can get through a hefty amount of burdens and trembling if you breathe – but it's not easy.

Maybe that's what my brother did. He lived a quiet life, never spoke of complaints. I wonder if he was concealing what troubled him. I can't know now. He didn't want anyone to know if something was amiss. That's just the way he was.

When they had a child born with setbacks, it had to have been sad and stressful, yet Douglas never complained. His answer to how his son was doing came swiftly, the boy was always fine. It was symbolic in many ways that the afflicted son died having physically grown to be a man. Three months later, Doug passed away, as if the duty of taking care of his child was completed. I never knew after that what happened to Doug's wife. She moved with no regard for leaving a new address. Sometimes you just need to let people go.

Suzanna

Wow, talking to my mother is becoming work. I almost feel like I'm bothering her, but someone needs to keep an eye on her.

Today I was so pleased to be welcomed into the environmental group. The first meeting is next week, and I'm going with ideas to present and a nice donation if it's appropriate. I believe in preservation of the land. The fires in this state are ghastly, the earthquakes frightening. The entire planet could use a little tenderness.

I hate the drilling on preserves, spoiling the pureness of the mountains, the forests, the streams. This group is admirable, and I'll be glad to take part in whatever it is they're currently involved with. It will be wonderful to feel part of something. How have I not recognized before this my need to be significantly useful?

What will Glenn think of my new interest? What do I care? I don't like the way I'm feeling about our marriage. He's disengaged – either he's away on business or he seems disinterested in doing the pleasant things we once enjoyed. He doesn't care about what I want. He doesn't want to consider painting the faded shutters a new color. He doesn't want to go out for dinner. Is he growing old and tired of what we once enjoyed?

Whatever he thinks of Green Space, he'll just have to get used to it. It won't affect him, and after all, he used to be the one of us who expressed his displeasure with the oil companies for their ocean spills and pipelines. What happened to that man? I feel that I've lost touch with Glenn on interests that drew me to him, that made him seem empathetic and engaging.

Speaking of engaging, after a strong cup of coffee, I'll call my children, maybe Kira first. Apparently it's not as much of an adjustment for them when they leave home for a chosen destination. There's excitement in change. It probably was the same for me. Moving to California was an adventure. It's the parents who get deserted.

Though I doubt that's what my father and mother felt when I chose college and marriage on the opposite coast. They had one another and the bustling city life to amuse them, so I'm certain they didn't miss me at all. Although Dad called me every couple of weeks, which is more than what my mother did. I think she may have been glad to get rid of me. I was always pretty independent.

So here I am, a few sips of coffee consumed. Kira's answering machine gracefully accepts my call, which may have been more than I'd expected. I leave a message that I have nothing specific to report but that she can give me a call if she wishes at her convenience. My God, do I know her anymore?

Jordan actually answers the phone. By the tone of his voice he seems worried, as if something is wrong and that's why I'm calling. When did calling become only a means of relaying bad news? Now that he knows I'm just checking in, he is his congenial self...that lasts about one minute, then he hurries me off the line because he needs to get to practice.

How have my children become strangers? When did time for family become a luxury too many can't afford? Sometimes I think about my cat and recall what good company she was. Someday I'm going to have another, whether Glenn approves or not.

All right, so this coming weekend if Glenn is still not home I'm going to the paint store. I'm painting the worn old shutters a new and vibrant hue, a forest green to match the new organization I'll soon be part of. And I may even buy myself a new pair of jeans, and maybe a new blouse or two. I've become a straight-edged dresser at work, always prim and proper. Once home, I'm into casual jersey pajama sets. Enough of that. I'll start wearing what I feel comfortable with, jeans and colorful tops.

* * *

Well, that was an interesting call. Glenn is flying in tomorrow. I mentioned briefly that I was getting involved with Green Space and he had no comment. Either he doesn't care or he thinks he'll change my mind. He does that when he doesn't like what I dream up, finds reasons why I should rethink a decision. Not this time. I'm enthused about doing something I regard as important, and no one is changing my plans.

Maybe I'll stop after work tomorrow and pick up the paint for the shutters. Once I've purchased it, Glenn can hardly dispute my willingness to brighten up the place. After all, I'm not asking him to do the painting.

With him being away so much of the time, I need to start taking charge of things – the house, the yard, my own existence. I never thought I'd find myself living alone in the woods, yet here I am.

I'm so damned proud of myself for having the gumption to add to my life without anyone else approving or disapproving. After all, I went from my parents' home to college to becoming Glenn's wife and Jordan's and Kira's mother. It's time for me to stand up for myself, to find *me*. Maybe I've been splintered too long, an insignificant sliver in the lives of my own family. Such a joke. What family am I thinking of? My dad is gone, my husband is hardly here, my son and daughter are like ghosts from the past, and my mother seems uncomfortable whenever I call. I am alone.

* * *

I bought the dark green paint after work, and I bought jeans and a watermelon colored shirt. I pulled into the driveway and saw Glenn's car and shivered. I wasn't sure why until I walked into the house and found him changing his clothing from the trip to chino pants and a sweater.

He greets me with a slight smile and a hello there. I looked at him, a husband who had been gone for nearly a month, and wonder why the moment was so lack-luster. He makes no move to approach me for even a kiss on the cheek. Nor do I. It feels as though I am looking at a stranger.

We say simple things to one another, about his trip and how things have been at home. We share a salad and rye toast with hummus. I make fresh coffee and we take it to the living room where he sits in his recliner and I settle in across from him on the sofa.

As I consider how to tell him of my plans – the shutter renewal, the environmental group – he starts to speak. He hesitates and I wonder if he's ill. He's been unrecognizably quiet in how he moves, how he barely consumed our light meal, and now how he's beginning to converse.

I sit silent, listening to what he has to say. When he's finished, I sit stunned, yet questioning my surprise. Why haven't I seen this coming? No, not another woman, another man; my husband and my son are both gay. How extraordinary for me not to suspect that there was anything at all different about either one of them. I question my own self-esteem, my sense of another's behavior. Did I not think to challenge Glenn or my awareness? My God, how did I not know? And further, am I so dense that Glenn looked at me as the perfect candidate to become his wife, to make him accepted in the work force, the community, his parents, his four brothers? Did they know? And if they did, what did they think of me for not having a clue?

I want to cry. I feel like I should. Yet I am numb. How does one respond to such news?

He looks so lost, so pained to have broken my heart. But he hasn't. I realize now that we never had a passionate or romantic love. We got along, found we fit well together, and that was it.

Tears are running down his cheek. I reach across and take his hand. I tell him that I think a part of me always knew, that everything will be okay, that I'll support him, that we'll figure it all out. I can tell he's relieved. As difficult as this is for me, I imagine it's more so for him.

We watch TV for a while, just to have a distraction. But there's definitely a tension present. After an hour, Glenn decides to go unpack, and he tells me he's going to sleep in Jordan's room. I'm relieved. He kisses me on the cheek goodnight.

After his footsteps have faded, I go to the kitchen and put our mugs in the sink then move to the bedroom. Just mine now.

Prone on my bed, staring at the patterned ceiling, I can't help but allow my mind to spin. We'd had what seemed to be a good marriage. We hardly ever argued. Maybe he just gave into me, to keep me around, part of the furniture in his life. Maybe I was just a part of the façade to look normal, to fit in at the company Christmas party. Or maybe he didn't know or wanted to hide the truth, even from himself.

If I had any friends, I might worry about what they'd think of this emotional circus, but I don't. I do wonder what my mother will say. My father would have been furious with Glenn, but my mother...I'm not sure I can ever tell her.

* * *

Somehow I managed to finally fall asleep last night, and I slept without dreams I can recall. Part of me hopes that last night was just a nightmare, but I know better.

I wonder if Glenn is still asleep in the room that once belonged to Jordan, and somehow I don't care if he's even there. I meant what I said last night, I'll support him. But who, I wonder, will support me? What are we to one another at this point?

I guess we'll sort through it all. I was feeling all alone anyway. There's a reason I decided to take action, to do something that's meaningful to me. I'm glad I'm meeting with the group at Green Space later today. I'm honoring that arrangement – for them and for me. I'll make myself valuable, an integral part of that respected community. Then again, I don't know yet what's going to happen.

As I go through the actions of selecting my outfit for today, sliding each hung garment in the closet from right to left, more scenarios play in my head. Glenn will probably be moving out. He may expect we'll sell this house. And then where will I go? Do I have any reason to stay here? Maybe I'll forfeit my job. Maybe I'll pay my mother a surprise visit. Or maybe I'll just move back there and stay so I can keep an eye on her. My God, why is so much askew in my life? At least my closet seems organized for a change. How ironic. The one area I could never keep to my mother's satisfaction is now the only thing she'd probably approve of.

Enough dragging my feet. I need to get ready for the day. And I need coffee. Glenn's either here or he's not.

I listen at the door and hear nothing, so I open it and move to the kitchen. There's coffee made, but no other sign of the man I married.

I'm walking around my house, cup of coffee in hand, looking for what has been lost. Glenn is nowhere to be found. His keys to the house are on the entry-way table. Next to his keys I set down the now cold mug from which I didn't even take a sip, and I look out the window. His car is gone from the driveway.

It's concerning that I haven't shed a single tear. When something is over, gone for all time, isn't it normal to mourn? We took vows. Everything we had built together, all of our dreams for the future, just gone, shattered.

Fragmented, in utter disrepair, this life never lived – not fully. I look back and wonder what I've missed out on over more than thirty years of marriage. I was never going to be who he wanted. What did we rob ourselves of? We had companionship. We cared for each other.

But neither of us had the opportunity to experience real love. Well, as far as I know. Maybe he found someone. Maybe that's why he finally told me. I really wish I knew when he figured all of this out. I'll need to call him later. For now, I need to get ready for my day.

As I drive, in spite of bright sun, the day seems to be covered in fog. I park and make my way inside to the monthly Saturday meeting, joining a group of about thirty environmental enthusiasts. I'm thankful that I dressed casually. They are welcoming. Brief introductions are made. While the agenda is covered, I realize that I'm looking forward to working side by side with these folks. It will be nice to work with people outside of social services – engineers, nurses, teachers, housewives, and one doctor. It's an informative and bright collection of people, all endeavoring to keep clean rivers flowing, garbage from the oceans, trees from being turned into logs, animals from being hunted. I finally feel like I belong, perhaps the first time in my fifty-three years.

Sadearah

Strange not to have had a call from Suzanna in more than a week. She's usually checking on me in her overbearing way. I suppose she's engaged in some social activity with her husband, or maybe one of her children paid them a visit. Who knows, and who cares? I guess I'm not going to win an award for being attentive to my only child's life.

Now that I've spoken to that nice Stephen down in Connecticut, our plans to meet for lunch tomorrow will be something to look forward to. I'll pack an overnight bag and stay at that little bed and breakfast near the farm just for one night, and I'll leave Georgie inside his home with plenty of hay and carrots hidden here and there. He'll be fine. I won't make a habit of going away from my funny friend. He does like to get outside in the fresh air, but I'll leave his window open. The screen will give him a cool breeze.

I wonder if I should call Suzanna before I leave in the morning. No, I can't do that. I'm leaving by seven and that's hours earlier in California. She wouldn't be at all happy about me waking her and Glenn while it's still dark outside their bedroom window. I don't know why she found it necessary to move so far away, but there's a reason I guess. I don't know what it is...suppose I never will. She obviously doesn't like me. I wish I knew why, but that's another thing I most likely will never understand.

Henry had the nerve to die and leave me with a difficult daughter. I'm doing okay though, especially since I have Georgie. And I'll be happy to be driving to Connecticut in the morning. I love seeing the farm even though it's owned by someone new, and having lunch with Stephen will be fun, too. He's such a nice fellow, might have been the type I'd have envisioned for Suzanna if given the chance. He's so different from Glenn. Probably one of many reasons why I like Stephen.

Suzanna

It should be interesting showing up at my mother's beach house without her knowing I'm arriving.

It feels liberating to have closed the house, booked this flight, and to have something other than Glenn to think about since meeting my Green Space people. I like them so much. Every one of them is dedicated to making this world cleaner, safer, renewed. Every time I mentioned my environmental concerns to Glenn over the years, he scoffed at my worries. He always asked what I thought I could do about it. I never had a good answer, but now I do. And maybe this will be a conversation I can actually have with my mother.

She always conserved water, was careful to recycle whatever she could, and urged Dad and me to use glass instead of plastic. I thought she was doing the right thing although I never said so. I really was difficult. I probably seemed unconcerned, or defiant for no real reason. Strange after all these years to recall the divisions we've had with one another. I'm tired of working so hard to stay apart.

* * *

Serves me right for not calling ahead. I'm standing in the sand at her door and her car is gone. Now what? Where could she have gone? Hopefully the key is in the same place we always kept it.

Walking to the shed, I notice the fence. There's evidence that something is using that area. There's bits of hay strewn about. And why does she have the door padlocked? There's nothing of value in there.

At least it requires a code, not a key. I bet its the same one we always used. Strange though – none of this was here the last time I was. But I'm thankful that the lock opens easily and the door doesn't stick…Good Lord Almighty! I close the door quickly then gather my wits. I'm not sure whether to laugh or cry or scream.

I push my way inside. Thank goodness the key to the house is at least dependably here. "And who might you be?" I ask the creature nuzzling his horns into my thigh. "Looks like, based on how much food she left, that it might be just you and me for a bit." I pet the old goat's head, grab the key, and work my way backwards through the door, making sure to secure the padlock. I shake my head and turn toward the house.

The Adirondacks are gone. She has a new bench in their place, looks like teak. I wonder why she got rid of the old chairs. Good grief, is everything different? My marriage is mangled, I've quit my job, and my mother has a goat.

I definitely need a cup of coffee. Maybe she has

something stronger I can have. It's been quite a week. But being here by the ocean is just what I need. That and for my mother to come home. Where would she go off to anyway?

It actually feels nice to be here alone for a change. Well, alone except for the goat. But I can see why my mother was drawn here.

It's after eight and the sun has dipped into the ocean, and here I am with a goat making noises in the shed. Maybe he's hungry. Damn, what do those things eat? From what I've heard, anything.

Come to think of it, I'm hungry too. I'll have to see what she has in the fridge. Not much, but enough. I know. I'll take him a cucumber and tomato sandwich. But with or without mayonnaise? I'm worried about whether a goat likes mayonnaise? I'll cut up an apple, too. Surely they eat apples. I'll make myself a sandwich too. Why not?

* * *

I'm worried. It's after midnight and there's no sign of my mother. What does she get up to when I'm not around? Obviously, she's decided to not confine herself. Maybe she went back toward Boston to see old friends. Though I can't imagine who. I think they're all dead. I don't know, but she'll certainly be surprised to see a bright blue rental car parked next to her house when she returns.

I'll give one last check on the goat to see if he ate the sandwich then I'll settle in for the night. I step outside and look at the stars, listen to the waves. My thoughts go first to my mother, wondering where she is, and then to my children. I wonder if they know yet about Glenn and if they will even care. Our lives have been disconnected for so long, and now I wonder if they sensed something was different and simply stayed away. I wonder if they'll blame me. My guess is they will.

Well, the shaky old flashlight allowed me to see clearly that the goat ate everything I gave him. Good, now I can relax until I fall asleep or my mother shows up. It is beyond aggravating that she just took off like this. She can't have gone too far. Then again, I didn't tell my kids that I was going anywhere, and here I am across the country. Wouldn't that be a hoot? If she decided to visit me when I decided to visit her? But we've never been that in sync. It couldn't happen. No, she's someplace else – probably someplace she'd much rather be than with me.

Suzanna and Sadearah

"For Heaven's sake, Suzanna! What are you doing here?"

I pull a sweater over my nightgown and stare at my mother as she walks in the kitchen door carrying an overnight bag.

"I'm about to have coffee. Perhaps you'd like a cup while you tell me exactly what you've been up to."

She set her overnight bag on a kitchen chair, and we face one another, standing just two feet apart.

"You never mentioned coming. What's going on?"

I look at her for several seconds, pour her a cup of coffee, then sit down at the kitchen table. "Where've you been?"

Mother sits down across from me and wraps her hands around her mug. Taking a deep breath she answers, "Young lady, I do not have to report to you about my comings and goings. I don't have to tell you everything that's going on in my life."

"What's his name?"

The look on my mother's face is one of shock. Maybe

she has a boyfriend. I hadn't thought of that before.

"Who's name?" she asks. "Do you mean Stephen?"

"Is that the name of the goat you have in Dad's shed?"

My mother bursts into laughter. "No, that's Georgie, and he is my pet. That's all you have to know about him."

"Okay. Well hopefully Georgie didn't mind mayo on his sandwich last night. Next, who's Stephen and where have you been?"

"As for where I've been, I went to the old farm. I felt the urge to be there again."

"You drove to Connecticut? By yourself?"

"Well the goat doesn't like long car rides. Yes, by myself. Now, suppose you tell me why you're here."

I sipped the hot coffee and looked from my mother's face to the French door, to the sand and wild growth before the ocean's surf. When I glance back at her I see an expression expecting a reply. "I'm here for a little visit."

"Why?"

I look away again, trying to dodge her question. Both of us are silent for several minutes, but when I look back to her alert eyes, I know there's no escaping the truth. My mother has always been an expert at patience. No pressure, just that intense ability to wait things out.

I look down at the cup in my hand, set it on the table, and push it away. "Glenn and I are no more."

Her silence is deafening. I finally look up at her. She

71

sits, statue still, with no reaction. I look at her and she at me. "Do you care to tell me more?" she asks.

I emotionally squirm, looking around at the pale yellow walls and then stare down at the cup I'd pushed away while I confess. "It seems my husband and I have something in common that I hadn't realized before. We're both interested in men."

Again there is silence. I can't stand the suspense any longer. I raise my eyes and my mother stares at me, uncomprehendingly. She must be wondering the same thing I've been: How could it be possible, after thirty years of marriage, not to know something so personal about your partner?

She takes a sip of coffee and simply says, "I see."

There are no signs of stress or question. I have no idea what she could be thinking. She's never questioned Jordan's lifestyle, although it's not necessarily a lifestyle – it's more what he is made of. I suppose that it's the same with Glenn. He didn't choose to be interested in the male over the female. Yet I can't stand that this impacts me…leaves me with so much uncertainty. I brush a tear away from my cheek.

"Are you alright?"

I nod. "I'm okay. Or, at least, I will be."

Had this conversation been with my father, there would have been questions, but my mother has always taken a back seat, watching and listening to my father and me.

My mother's eyes are focused on mine. "Okay. Well,

if there's anything else you want to tell me, I'm here."

That's the way it was with her, always. My father would have demanded the details. I look toward the French door again and then at my mother. "I just don't know how I could have been so blind to it all."

My mother's expression doesn't change. Her eyes seem a bit glossy, but she doesn't flinch.

I stand and take my cup to the sink, empty it, rinse it out, then fill it with fresh coffee. "Will you have some more?"

"Yes, I think I will."

We sit with our hot drinks and are quiet. It's awkward but now it's out, a secret no longer kept.

"Do you have any plans?"

I looked at my mother and shook my head. "At this point, just to survive."

"You will."

Again there was silence. My dad would have asked what I intended.

"So tell me about the goat."

My mother sipped her coffee and looked at me with a softness I don't recall seeing before. "Georgie is a pet. I help out at a local goat farm once in a while. Sometimes I assist in making cheese. Georgie is an older fellow. He was harassed a bit by the younger males. They were going to sell him, so now he lives with me."

"Why didn't you tell me? He wasn't here the last time I visited."

My mother's lips cracked into a flicker of a smile.

"Or was he?" I asked.

"I didn't think you'd approve, so for the length of your stay, I had him taken back to the farm."

Another secret kept from me. "So he's a permanent resident here?"

"Yes."

"And you stayed overnight in Connecticut."

"Yes. I left here yesterday morning, stayed overnight, and woke this morning at four. I decided to hit the road for home, and here I am, three and a half hours later. If I'd known you were here to give Georgie fresh water and food, I might have stayed there longer."

I look at the earnest expression, her words delivered without regret.

"What does he eat?"

"Goat food, a mix I buy at the grain store. And pretty much anything else in small portions."

"I gave him a sandwich and an apple last night. I haven't been out to feed him yet this morning."

"I'm sure he was grateful."

I stand and walk to the sink where I leave my empty cup. I stare out through the kitchen window to sea meadows blowing in the soft morning wind. "You have no intention of leaving here do you?"

"None whatsoever," she says. "I would have lived here years ago, but your father preferred the city. I was lucky he consented to living here summers. And you, will you remain in California?"

I take a deep breath and face her. "For now, yes. The

74

plan is to sell the house, hopefully furnished – I don't want anything, and maybe move to a condo. Glenn signed the house over to me. He's moving to Japan."

I can tell she has questions, but unlike my father, she is quiet, waiting.

"I've resigned from my job and can sit on my laurels for eternity. Money isn't an issue."

Still, no reaction.

"I'll keep myself busy with Green Space."

Her expression changes, her eyebrows slightly raised. "Green Space? You're working with them?"

"Yes. I've always cared about what was being destroyed through huge corporations dumping waste into our waters, toxins blown ruthlessly into the atmosphere, pipelines cutting through prime lands. It needs to be stopped."

We look at one another in silence.

I know exactly what she's thinking, that for some unknown reason I've taken her lead and am following in her footsteps. She'd worked for years to put a check on unfiltered smoke from factory chimney stacks, and she'd tirelessly concerned herself with water filtration and new pipes in Boston. I'm sure she had no idea that any of that rubbed off onto me.

"How are Kira and Jordan?"

I smile. She's avoiding talking more about my plans and this is her way of discovering how her grandchildren are taking this new development.

"Fine, I suppose. To my knowledge, they haven't yet

been told about their father. At least it wasn't my place to tell them. But I'll call them when I go home. I expect it to be a surprise, but maybe they guessed long ago and I'm the stupid one."

"You're far from stupid, Suzanna."

I shake my head. "I'm not so sure of that. Decades with a man and didn't know his preference for his own sex. At first, I listened to him feebly explain the deception and wondered if I had not been enough for him. A little more thought to the subject convinced me that no woman could have filled the gap he was missing. I was just the excuse to appear like a typical family."

After sitting still for a few moments, my mother stands and announces she's going out to the shed. "When I've fed Georgie and let him out into the paddock, I'll be in to take a quick shower. I thought I might fix some eggs and sliced watermelon. Georgie would like some of the melon as well. Any interest in some food?"

I nod, suddenly feeling starved. "Yes, that actually sounds good."

"Alright then. Why don't you go have a seat on the new bench? The Adirondacks had had it. Your father's chair broke and the other was fairly decayed. I'll bring breakfast outside for us. The air is wonderful this morning."

Without a word, and in my nightdress and bare feet, I do as suggested, my eyes to the rolling surf. I'm not sure why, but suddenly I need to cry. I've been too angry to shed tears before. I sit down on the bench, the sorrow engulfs me.

Sadearah

With Suzanna gone I feel free to let my tears stream down onto my sun-bathed face. It's so difficult when your child suffers and there's nothing you can do. But at least she felt like she could come here, come to me. And she definitely likes Georgie and he her. But now she's gone.

This is the same loneliness I felt when Henry died. Suzanna will face that emotion as well when she gets back home, even though hers will be laced with anger and questions. Surely she is mourning the loss of an incomplete union, the loss of what could have been.

Oh, Henry, why aren't you here to help us through this? I look to the sky and wonder where the spirit goes when one passes.

My greatest wish, before I pass, is that my child finds contentment. I wonder if the environmentalists will manage to fill her empty hours. I hope so – it's a good cause. Maybe she will even meet someone there. A friend or something more eventually.

But now she has gone back and needs to face her

children. I worry about their reaction. Will they support their mother? Will they support their father? Will they just shrug their shoulders and go about their lives? I really wish I knew them better. I have no sense of what they will do.

What I do know is that Glenn is lucky that he's in Japan. If I were to run into him, I'd tell him he was a selfish human to take a woman's life so casually. And I wouldn't be nice about it either. Poor Suzanna. She blames herself, but there's nothing a person can do to fight their nature.

I can't help but think of my visit to the farm in Connecticut, the rolling hills, the span of meadows filled with thick green grass, bordered with huge maples. I love it there, but I love it here as well, and I can manage this small house. I do think Georgie would love it there though, plenty of room for a goat to romp about, but maybe at his age he's beyond romping and glad to be comfortable. Sort of like me, I'm content with this place.

Apparently I too am growing old, and I question how and what I think. In my mother's final years, I was always on alert for her often confusing words and her impulsive steps to walk to the door and out into the winter snows. I had to watch her every move, fearful she'd get up in the night and we'd find her frozen to the ground by morning. Henry scoffed at her behavior, telling me to put her in a home where she'd be safe and I'd be at peace. His own parents died in a medical facility, none of their children helping them to remain at home. I mentioned once that they could stay with us or we could stay with them. No, Henry was adamant that a facility could best handle their needs. My mother died in her own bed, in her own home, with my hand over hers.

I'm not going to think of this anymore right now. I'm going to think of the lovely day I had in Connecticut and the very nice luncheon I had with Stephen. He was so welcoming to me and, while I don't know his age, I do think he's younger than Suzanna. Perhaps he's forty-five or six, somewhere in there. It doesn't matter. We had a nice conversation and he welcomed me to call him when I will be visiting the old farm again. Maybe in October when the leaves will be brilliant out in the Berkshires.

Next time she comes to visit, I should see if Suzanna wants to go with me. I can't imagine what she's going through in rearranging her once orderly life – giving up that big home in the redwoods, moving to a condo. And Glenn is moving to Japan. I wonder if the man he cares for is Japanese. I thought of asking Suzanna but decided not to. If Henry was here, he'd ask. He'd scold Glenn's deceit and probably scold his daughter for not recognizing a deception. Who would suspect such a thing? I doubt I'd have noticed if a man was clever and treated me as though I mattered. Henry treated me well even though he likely thought of another. Suzanna must have felt content enough as I did.

I think of Henry more now than when he first died. With the brand new emptiness, I was willing to give him a pass on what he had insisted upon. After all, his life

80

was gone. As time passes, I question more, and I wonder if divorce works in a similar way. I'm not pleased with myself for resenting some of what Henry dictated. I have a mind and a tongue. I could have given Henry a refusal now and then. I wonder how he'd have handled that from me.

I've never been particularly vindictive, even with my mother calling me that terrible name, but I do find myself regretting some of what I let others in my life get away with. It bothers me, and I so wish it didn't, that Henry loved someone before me and that maybe what he felt for me was a simple acceptance, a second choice. I am Sadearah, and I've been a decent person all my life, and I'm a damn good tender of goats.

Suzanna

The gang at Green Space is just what I needed, and given my ability with office manager qualities, they are excited to rope me in. I've told them that while I am happy to be of help with computer-oriented projects, I also want to be out in the field, cleaning our brooks, or whatever else they choose to tackle. I want to wear my green sweatshirt with the proud name of our organization, and I want it to get dirty.

With my steaming mug of coffee in hand I think of how I'd like to take it outside in the pre-autumn air, sun streaking through the redwoods, a light breeze. Unfortunately we have no outside furniture. Glenn always said the birds could "Christen" it and he was a bit of a germaphobe. My mother has it right with her nice teak bench. She can have lunch out there if she wishes. Once the house is sold, and there are so many aspects of it I'll miss, I'll find a condo with a terrace or balcony for outdoor savoring of food and drinks. It's time for me to reinvent myself, something I never thought of before Glenn's proclamation of desire for another.

This weekend I'll search for a place, something not too big, and where if I want something as a pet, maybe a cat again, I can have one. It would be nice to come home from being out all day to a living creature, something glad to see me. Lord knows I haven't experienced that in a while.

I should call my mother this evening, maybe around seven her time. I'll probably catch her feeding the goat. She never fails to surprise me. Nothing could have prepared me for discovering her choice in a companion. And then her journey to Connecticut, all that way by herself. I don't know what she's thinking – anything could have happened to her. It might have been a very resourceful move for me to show up on the Cape without giving her a clue I'd be there. Some of what she does mystifies me, and I would guess that with age it won't get easier.

She does seem to be handling life alone fairly well. My father was one who took control and she let him. He decided what we were having for supper, and sometimes he cooked it. Other times he would select an item my mother fancied making – spaghetti and meatballs, meatloaf, roasted potatoes with scallions around layers of chicken. We dined well, always something nutritious and tasty.

Glenn never cooked, never suggested a meal. I did the cooking, decided what to serve, and he ate it without comment. The more I think of my thirty year union, the more I feel left out and underappreciated by both husband and children.

* * *

I can't believe I've found a place to live without intentionally looking for one. The bungalow down the street had a *for sale* sign on it today. To think I drove past that little house every day on my way to work and never gave it much thought. I'd see an older man outside tending to a little garden, a small white dog at his heels. On a whim, I went past then turned my car around, stopped, and took a good look. After calling my real estate broker and her meeting me there, I decided it was home. It needs cosmetic help, but with time, I can handle that.

The yard is a never-ending acre of weeds, but it's sunny and open, no big trees shading the rooms. The kitchen is modest with a wood-top island scarred from years of a careless knife and hot pans. I don't care – it shows life, something I seem to have missed before now. I'll paint the walls and have the electric and plumbing updated. And now I'll have a pet, that little white dog, Casper, has been living in the house – someone coming to care for him daily. With his master deceased, he'll need something consistent, and he'll have his home. His name is very suiting for his ghostly shade. I'm so glad they accepted my offer. Now I just need one on my house. Yes, this is my house, but that will be my home.

I can't help smiling at my new adventure into solitary

home ownership. Glenn wouldn't approve of the funky little place. It's so different from the posh setting that's held me for so long. And it's certainly different from where I was raised with city life. This will be a new experience, a new life. An actual life. It will likely surprise those who know me. It wasn't what I'd expected either. I'd pictured myself in a modern condo. Something easy, with no maintenance. Instead I'm going to become more proficient at taking care of my home and myself.

I'll eat grilled cheese sandwiches for supper when I want to, and I'll have cold pineapple slices for breakfast. When Glenn was around, we had to have eggs, toast, the works. Not anymore. I'll do as I wish. Now I have something to tell my mother and my children when I call them. I think they're going to be surprised.

It will take me a couple of weeks to sort out if there's anything I want from the house. I should ask the kids if there's anything they want too. Otherwise I'll plan to leave most of the furnishings behind or have some company come in to take it all away. Glenn already said he wants nothing, the move to Japan will be kept simple.

* * *

Kira and Jordan didn't sound upset with the news of Glenn and I parting. It seems like they already knew. And, big surprise, they want nothing from the house. I'm not sure I do either. Maybe I'll start fresh with choices of my own.

Tonight I'll call and check in on my mother, let her

know that I'm moving to the bungalow in a couple of weeks. In telling her, I'll be swallowing a certain amount of pride. I've wondered how she could move from our large house in Jamaica Plain to a four-room cottage on the Cape. Yet here I am, doing the same with a four-room bungalow, an unruly garden, and a tiny white dog eleven years old.

Casper and I will live a happy life. I'll invite friends over for coffee or a nice meal without worrying about anyone else's approval. And I can go out as I please too. Already Mia has asked me out for coffee, Joe the same, and Curt and Diane Martinez have told me to stop by their home anytime. I'm not sure I've ever felt this type of acceptance from others before, not this much.

I wonder if my mother has people she has coffee with. Or maybe she feels isolated since Dad died. She's there at that cottage most of the time alone. She had friends when we lived near Boston. She was involved with everything from the homeless shelters to the museums. I remember wondering why she put herself out that way, and here I am, an excited new member of Green Space, with people of my own sort. It feels comfortable. Maybe that's why she goes and helps out at the goat farm. And why she has her Georgie. He's such a sweet creature, and quite the character too. Tonight I will make the call, I will expect a non-judgmental reply from her when I explain about my bungalow, and I'll fish for how she's managing with autumn on its way and her seemingly solitary life.

Sadearah

The call from Suzanna was expected since I hadn't heard from her in several days. She was once so concerned about me living on my own that I could count on hearing from her every three days. I think she thought I was fairly incapable without Henry to do my bidding. He was intent on being in charge, so I let him. Every time I think of Henry, I associate him with the large house we shared in Jamaica Plain. He was impressed with the size of the rooms and the quantity of them, ten, which were more than we needed. I wasn't unhappy there – it was a lovely place, but when he died, I knew it was far too much for me. This cottage is perfect.

Now my daughter, who tries hard to be so different from her mother, is doing the same. She thought of herself in a posh condo yet she's buying a little old bungalow with a resident dog. I smile at the thought.

She seemed rather surprised, at least she was silent for a few moments, when I told her I thought the change was going to be wonderful for her. A new start, an independent life she is well-equipped to handle. What I said to her was the absolute truth. Suzanna is a capable woman. Her life is in her hands and that's the best place.

I held back a gurgle of laughter as she told me she might have a shed put on the property similar to mine. I choked back the urge to ask if she was thinking of getting a goat. In my silence, she told me she wanted to have a little garden and the shed would be a great place to leave a wheel barrow, a rake, a shovel of some sort. I complimented her inspiration to garden, to promote life on her land. I reminded her gently that becoming part of Green Space was an honorable thing to do. Without over-complimenting her, I expressed my approval whether she wanted it or not. My daughter is a stable, strong person. She's going to be okay.

I sit here sometimes with the phone in my hands as though I'm still connected to her. If Henry had been here, he would have taken the call and asked a million questions regarding Glenn, the kids, and Suzanna's new endeavors. He probably would have admonished her for quitting her job, and maybe for leaving her large home. But Henry isn't here, and while I miss aspects of him quite often, I also feel a relaxation in knowing that I can do whatever I want to do whenever I want to do it. On the phone I felt that resolve in Suzanna, that she was in a solid place where she can get on with her life using her own good sensibilities.

I wonder, too, about Glenn. After thirty years with a wife and children, a nice home and a respectable position, how is he going to manage life in a country where he has only visited? Living in a new place is not always an easy adjustment. I wonder, too, if he worries about how his son and daughter accepted his rather selfish move. He'd kept the secret for so long, and while I can't judge him as Henry definitely would have, I do wonder how he justifies the havoc he's created. He was a take-charge person like Henry, refined and kind to us as his in-laws. I can only hope he made the right move for everyone because certainly he's tipped over a barrel of pickles.

Sometimes we find good things at the bottom of the barrel though. Suzanna certainly seems like she's on a happier path. She's capable, smart, and while I wish she hadn't chosen to be so far away, she's mapped out a life, even in her present stress. I remember when she fell off a boy's bike at age eight, skinning her knees, blood dripping down to her feet. She came into the house with a tear-stained face, wiping evidence dry with her forearm, the only part of her anatomy that hadn't been scrapped. I thought to console her as I cleaned the areas affected and left ointment and bandages in place. She never said ouch, and she didn't flinch. This was a girl who wasn't going to give in, not for anything. Now I think of her as a woman with grown children of her own and wonder how she's managed to keep those emotions so tight to her heart. I think I should thank Glenn. Maybe my daughter will have a chance to find real love, a love that is truly meant for Suzanna. Everyone deserves that. Except me, I'm too stubborn to conform to another at this point in my lovely life.

It always comes back to Henry. Sometimes I look at his old desk and wonder why I brought it here. It's all I took from the old house when it was sold. There simply isn't room for more. We already had the rooms furnished, but I made room for the desk here in the kitchen. It's a little tight, but I like seeing the rich cherry wood and the curved legs. It's a bit out of fashion with the other simple pieces in this cottage, but I don't care. I could not abandon the one piece of furniture he cherished, perhaps more than he cherished me.

I wonder how my life would have differed if I'd refused his proposal and spent my life with someone else. There's no way to know what would have, could have been. I had a crush on Jimmy Hale all through high school, but he never knew it. He was the star player on the basketball team, and I pretended not to care when he waved to me from the center of the court. I later heard that he married and died at the age of thirty-six due to a blood clot in his heart. That would have finished me. I still think of him. What I felt for Jimmy wasn't love though. For love, you have to really know someone, not just imagine what or who they are.

I knew and cared for Henry. He was tall and handsome, a confident man who told me what to do and I did it. I had never responded to anyone like that before – usually I was quick to say no without a reason, but Henry wasn't good at accepting no. I stopped saying that little word and gave in to his irresistible poise. Maybe I shouldn't have. While no one in particular captured me completely, I regret that I never felt immense love. I protected my heart from being broken – never giving anyone a chance to know me. I guess I was afraid no one would like the real me. My mother certainly didn't seem to. I've wondered about my motives for being mum, but it's a bit too late to rectify the past.

What I need to do now is concentrate on living and loving my moments. Everyone is aware that age gets you closer to the grave, but the fact remains, none of us, at any age, is spared by sudden darkness. I don't think about dying. Like Emily Dickenson's "Because I could not stop for death," I really don't have time for it. I have Georgie depending on me, and while Suzanna may think she doesn't need a mother, I'm here, and she came here, to me, when she needed a place to feel safe, a person to be there for her. I intend to be what she needs from me. I won't make a move to California, and I've been waiting for her to suggest just that. Sorry, Suzanna, not going. Maybe now that she'll have the bungalow and the dog and Green Space, she'll give up trying to micromanage me from three thousand miles away.

When our phone call ended and the silence lingered, I wondered what Suzanna would do at that moment. I suppose she might have gone to bed. Or maybe she ran a warm bath, dreaming of her new bungalow and the first time she would live alone. I wonder if she'll take to that as I did. I had my worries here and there, a little noise outside, howling wind that might bring down a tree or wires leaving me in the dark. I did lose power a couple of times, once for three days, but I managed. I lit candles and made tea on my reliable old gas stove. I survived. And what would Henry have done if he'd been here during those times? He couldn't have restored the power. We'd have been here in the dark together, with Henry fuming over the inconvenience or insisting we go back to the city.

Tomorrow I'll head to the hardware store and stock up on batteries for my lantern in case the September winds decide to be bossy. I'll prepare my pantry with foods easy to heat – soups, maybe some hash and baked beans. Last year I had no emergencies, no harsh winter to test my fortitude. My second year here I was over confident and that's when the power outage was a test. I passed. I didn't have Georgie then, but I can manage him if I lose the lights and heat. I'll bring him into the kitchen. The walls are thicker than the shed, he'd have me for company, and we can use the hearth for heat.

I'm not sure why I torment myself with what ifs. The power may not be tested, but there's nothing wrong with being prepared. I need to practice not being negative so much. Henry used to remind me to be more positive and I thought he was full of it, or himself. I was frightened of thunder and lightning. He was right to suggest we were safe, and now when a storm comes near, I sit down with a hot cup of something and dare the violent elements to frighten me. They do, but I sit stoically, resisting the urge to tremble. I can do this.

Suzanna

The call to my mother tonight was different than I expected. I thought she'd have guarded opinions on my bungalow and that she'd be loaded with questions about how everything was going regarding the divorce. She asked me nothing. My father would have interrogated me and offered, no insisted, suggestions. I would have had to think quickly for proper replies.

My mother was listening to me, which I might not have noticed before. She asked only about the color of my new abode and when I'll move there. I told her the bungalow is kind of a bright blue, but that my intention is to paint the exterior light gray, the trim white, all of which will be done after I move in after we pass papers in a week. She replied that she liked gray because it's a neutral color, easy to look at. I wonder if she would have voiced an opinion if I told her I was painting the house purple. Probably not.

She asked, too, about Casper, and said that he was a lucky little soul. I thought about that for a moment, the little soul part. My mother has a passion for caring for creatures – she believed we all should.

I sit back in Glenn's recliner and close my eyes. It's strange to think that this is probably one of the last times I'll sit where his body had so often relaxed while he read or watched TV. I don't care though. My life with him is over, and I haven't felt stressed or abandoned with his move to Japan. He was so often gone anyway. He wasn't who I thought he was. But we had a decent life together while it lasted. Lately, though, I've been wanting something more. Maybe I knew that neither of us could be what the other wanted any longer. Maybe we never were.

Glenn and I didn't discuss it, but I wonder if he had always known, if our marriage had started as a charade. Had I been lied to so effectively? What's wrong with me that I had no idea that my husband didn't enjoy our lives as a married couple? The pretending must have been a nightmare for him. I wonder now if that's why we were gradually dismissed from the companionship of former friends. Maybe they observed what I missed.

I can't keep retracing the past. I have a new home and Casper to love and an involvement with an organization I believe in. I'm making new friends, and my mother seems adept at handling her life for the moment. I'll sneak a trip back there in a month or so to make sure her actions are making sense. I'm a little concerned about the goat, how she's going to handle him as time goes by. I wonder if she has plans for someone to help her care for him if that becomes necessary.

It's after eleven. Revisiting the words my mother and I shared has tired me out. I think she's okay, and I think I'm okay. I need to be – there are no choices. Everything is coming together: the house is sold, the bungalow bought, I'm now part of Green Space, and there's the prospect of new companions. No exaggerated shopping excursions with people I once thought of as friends. Some of those women had nothing in common with me nor I with them. There was an elaborate pretense going on to have a warm body to hang out with.

It's wildly different at Green Space. The interest is genuine. I've been invited to join their quest for a healthier environment, and I've been invited to join them for socializing as well. I'm not sure I've ever felt this acceptance before now. Maybe, possibly, Glenn has done me a great favor by leaving. He and I may have opportunities for fulfillment, and maybe even for happiness. I think I've missed that somehow.

I was thinking I'd take a nice shower, but maybe not tonight, maybe in the morning. I find myself counting the number of times I will do this or that in this house for the last time. I think about the last pot of coffee, the last time I see the deer wandering through the woods, the last time I flip off the lights, forever. This house holds many memories. First steps, first words from my children.

Holidays were always cheerful. I think back to the Christmas lights and the tree being decorated with beautiful ornaments and pine cones dipped in glue and glitter. I remember the toys everywhere and how much Jordan loved climbing the low branches of the front yard pine. He called it *his* tree because most of what we had were the redwoods. Kira decided at six that if Jordan was keeping the pine to himself, she was having all the redwoods. No one argued the point with her, and now she won't see them again. She's chosen city life, kind of like me choosing California over Massachusetts. And with that thought, I wonder if I chose California or if I chose to be as far away as I could from my parents, from their tightness of two that I never could quite squeeze into. I guess I don't know the answer to that mystery. I'm exhausted. I need my bed.

Sadearah

Every time I wake up and see a day like this, filled with sunshine and soft air, I'm reminded of the responsibility I feel for living my best.

I will make a pot of coffee, get dressed, tend to Georgie, then make myself a plate of scrambled eggs with the last of summer's tomatoes chopped in with a bit of cheddar cheese. I'll skip the toast, but eggs and coffee will be scrumptious. Georgie will certainly appreciate some sliced apples and watermelon to go with his feed. He'll have the run of the paddock as well as his shed, freedom to do as he chooses, just like me.

As I move through my day, I can't help but think of my daughter. This being alone stuff is new to her, and while she sounds brave and propelling ahead on the phone, I wonder and hope all at the same time that she's truly content.

There are so many things I never shared with her, things like the doubts I had about marrying her father, or getting married at all for that matter. I wasn't sure I wanted to share a bathroom with anyone. That thought alone often turned me into an old maid. I wasn't interested in picking up or cleaning after another human being. I'd have had a pack of dogs or a collection of cats, but humans were not all that appealing. And there were my feelings, or lack of feelings, for my parents. They weren't terrible people, but they seemed absent to me. And after my mother called me that name, just because I was trying to soothe the relationship between her and my sister, any love I had for her dissipated.

Esther never knew that I'd been in trouble because of her. I doubt she'd have cared. She was self-centered, but so pretty that many of her negative aspects were forgiven. I always wondered what life must have been like for someone who looked in the mirror and saw that well-arranged face. Not that I was or am ugly. I was purposely plain. I didn't try to attract the boys. I saw what that had done to my sister and wanted no part of the turmoil, the crying, the questioning about why a relationship didn't work out. Even when I was twelve I could have told her not to be so agreeable with the boys, not to stand so close to them when they talked on the sidewalk. I don't think Esther would have listened to me though.

When she told me she was marrying Tom, I was horrified. I was fifteen, she was nineteen. I thought Tom was a jerk. Good looking as he was, there was something mean about his eyes, and I worried that he wouldn't really love my sister. I was right – he didn't. He caused her too much agony to have really loved her.

I don't feel distressed and that's a gift. Emotionally I've always been protective of myself. Physically, I've never been afraid of hard work, but I never took many risks there either. My knees are a little stiff, but not bad. I know people younger than me who are in poor shape. I'm grateful as well as cognizant that I could find myself fading at some point, but I can't worry about what might be in the future.

I need to stop pondering on the past too. But as the eggs cook, my thoughts drift back to growing up with Doug, seven years my senior, and beautiful Esther. I considered myself comfortable with life, in need of nothing, but what else could I think when that was all I knew? And it made me who I am, taught me to be proficient, to seek a strong education, to feel fulfilled, enjoy my own company. My youth had gifted me with independence and the ability to entertain myself whereas poor Esther went from one relationship to the next, always looking to someone else for acceptance, for love. Losing her baby had to have been her personal horror. She had knitted both a blue and a pink sweater and booties in rainbow colors. I wonder what she did with them.

I take my breakfast out to the bench and sit down to enjoy the sea air. The eggs are good, not great, but, still, nutritious. I think I may not have salted and peppered them enough and I'm too lazy to go back into the house for more. I'll sit here in the sun for a while and then maybe take a walk on the shoreline. If I were down in

Connecticut, maybe I'd have coffee with Stephen and then walk in the meadows. But I'm here on the Cape, which I love as much as Connecticut's hills.

How lucky I am to live on my own, to have Georgie, to be able to drive myself back to warm memories, and to have a good friend like Stephen to visit. I am undaunted. Only a spell of bad health can take me down, and only for a little while. When the flu hit me last year, I managed. The shot kept the symptoms low while tea and light food fed my energy level. Of course, I didn't have Georgie then. I'll need to talk to Kate, see if she's willing to help me out with him should there ever be a need.

Standing now, I can see Georgie nibbling on the low pine branches. He makes me laugh. All the nice food I gave him this morning and he wants the pine boughs. I wonder if his mouth gets sticky.

No question that this plate will be difficult to wash if I leave the remnants of my breakfast to set any longer. Time to put these dishes in the sink to soak in warm water and suds, then I'll head to the beach.

When I get back from my walk, I'll have a little visit with my spunky friend. Maybe I'll put his leash on him and go to the water. Every now and then he walks with me to the waves, hesitant to allow the salt water to curl around his feet. I laugh at the look on his face, the raised head as the ocean wins, and I watch as he backs up where he can feel the moist sand beneath his hooves. I try to ease his concerns about drowning in the six-inch surf, but I lose, and always, I urge him back toward the shed and the safety of his paddock area. He's dear to me, a sweet animal who fathered many and then feared the younger males as they romped boisterously too close.

I always wonder when I decide to nap or go to bed for the night if everyone else is as lucky as I am. What more could I ask for than what I have, the realization that every moment is a promise for more joy, and if that joy is taken through injury or illness, the recollections remain. I have grand memories, and I refuse to forget them. I may grow older, but I won't lose myself in the process. I just won't. My hope is that my daughter will retain the good from her marriage. After all, it had its delights, happy times with their children, days in the park with picnics. She must remember these things always. They're part of who she is.

Now, where did I leave my plastic pail? I may find shells and pretty stones to add to my collection.

Suzanna

Handing the key over to the new owners, the idea of it, is far more devastating than I imagined it could be. Turning out of the driveway for the last time, I'm reminded of how much I always liked the crunching sound of the gravel beneath my tires. While this is the end of so much, I must keep in mind that it is also the beginning of something that could be – no, will be – spectacular.

As I drive to the office where the closings will take place, I think about the plain hard-packed dirt driveway to the bungalow. I could have sizable rocks delivered to create a border on each side, then have the twenty or so feet filled with gravel.

* * *

I drive by my new home to pick up Casper from his grooming appointment. While there, I'll buy him a soft bed and a few toys. I didn't notice any around. But I'm sure he'll be happy to return to his familiar world. He must wonder what happened to his good friend.

Abandonment is a very strange feeling. I can relate.

While I don't feel the deep emotions I thought I might when Glenn was actually gone, out of the country, there's a sense of loneliness lingering around.

With Casper's leash in one hand and a bag of goodies in the other, his new bed under my arm, we leave the store and head home.

Pulling into my new driveway has its rewards along with the sorrows. I see the house as it will be when I've given it a cosmetic lift, yet somehow I feel that I said goodbye to a dear friend in leaving my old home. I can't help but recall the exhilarating feeling when we walked into that beautiful space for the first time. I knew it was ours, that it was destined to be the origin for great enjoyment. The house didn't fail. We did.

Inside the bungalow I half smile and half cry. It looks worn from age and neglect, and I'm feeling a bit of that myself. Leaving my jacket on a chair, I unclip Casper's leash and place it next to the fireplace. I touch the mantel and find a layer of dust. Everything will need some attention, and except for an old sewing machine in an attractive wooden stand, and one rocking chair made of some sort of fruitwood, I plan to donate the rest of the furnishings.

I imagine the living room with a comfortable sofa and two nice chairs, maybe something in a shade of cinnamon, and a nice oriental rug with brilliant red tones for the wide pine floors. I'm going to make this place mine. Perhaps I'll find some antique pewter pieces and candles to set on the dark wooden mantel.

Casper and I will enjoy a good fire on crispy evenings. The fireplace looks like it hasn't been used recently – maybe that's a good thing. I should get the chimney inspected and cleaned. There's so much to do.

I decide to make a list of items to address, another list of items to purchase. I take a pen and paper from my pocketbook and write *fireplace*. Walking into the kitchen, I make note of the cracked window pane. I have no idea how to replace the broken glass, but I'll find a handyman somewhere to help out with these minor adjustments. I didn't expect an old house lived in by an elderly man to be faultless.

The house, like me, just needs a little love. I feel wilted, very much alone. It's not so much that I miss Glenn or even my children. I think I miss myself. I'm not sure where I went to in my youthful decisions to leave everything I knew for something that was simply different. Now I long for something familiar, comfortable.

Good grief, I forgot to pick up more dog food at the store. At least I'm familiar with the area. I'll head to the local grocery mart for a few basics and dog food. When I get back, I'll make up the bed, which belonged to the former owner, and I'll put on some music while I eat then start to unpack. There's no TV here, so I'll buy one tomorrow and have it hooked up. Gradually I'll buy new beds for my room and the guest room, and I'll buy the living room set. The kitchen table and four chairs are sturdy and clean. I think I'll keep them.

* * *

Casper has gone from room to room. Even after all this time, I'm sure he's in search of his master. I keep calling to him, offering him food, even a small piece of cheese. He sniffed it, looked at me, then wandered around again. How do I explain to him that everything except the house has changed? If there's one thing I have in common with my mother it's worrying about animals and their feelings.

Casper and I will become friends. I understand this, yet he might not. I'll prove to him that we can be happy out on walks and sharing cozy evenings at home. These will be two of our main sources of pleasure now, one another and this small house.

Once settled in, I'll gradually make changes in colors to the walls. I want it light, a soft white everywhere with accent colors for each room. I'll do my own room – the curtains, the rugs – with hues in green. I'll do the guest room with accessories in blue. I'll add touches of red to the kitchen, and the living room will be as I first thought, a warm shade of tan with a plush red oriental rug. This is going to be home, and what I'm not so sure of is that the house I left in the redwoods was *ever* home. It was a remarkable place on equally remarkable land yet devoid of emotion from its inhabitants. Again, it was not the fault of the structure, but the human defects. I hope that its new owners fill it with love.

One week from today is Jordan's birthday, and three weeks later is Kira's. I'll need to pick up a couple of cards. I've given up on buying gifts, they never seem to care for what I've selected. The past couple of years I tuck a check into the envelope with the greeting and wish them a happy day.

Now that I think of it, I probably was ungratefully selective with my own parents' gifts to me. One year, I think it was my second year of college, they sent me a pink sweater that reminded me of a flamingo. I would never have worn such a thing. My roommate liked it and it ended up being her favorite piece of clothing. She had compliments from guys and gals alike when she wore it, which made me question my own taste. I'm also not sure I ever remembered to thank my parents for that gift. They had included a check which I probably spent on margaritas and tight fitting jeans. Who knows? It was a long while ago.

I miss my dad. He was a little on the bossy side, but when I think of his advice over the years, most of it was for my benefit, not his. I wonder what he would have thought knowing that Glenn abandoned us. That word, abandon, shocks me that I even thought of it. I hadn't felt abandoned when he told me he was leaving. I felt numb. But now I feel abandoned. After thirty years with someone, it seems impossibly rude to just leave them. I question what I did wrong, and then I remind myself that his decision wasn't about me. Maybe I was wrong to have not listened to my parents, to have married Glenn. He was very persuasive and I was apparently mindless. I guess it felt good to have someone solid, confident, easy to be around who wanted me.

* * *

I've been in this house for nearly a week and just today the repair was completed on my broken kitchen window. The chimney was checked, cleaned, and is now ready for a nice warm glow in the hearth. Some chilly night Casper and I will sit and enjoy the ambience on our new furniture. I like this place. I still feel a bit disconnected, like a baby cut from the umbilical cord, floating free and a little uncertain. I believe I can make my new life work. I have confidence in my future, in me. Maybe I'll offer to host one of the Green Space committee meetings – a small one, but that would be fine. I've missed entertaining, and this inspiring group of people make good things happen. My involvement with them is just what I need. Why didn't I realize this before?

Sadearah

The first chill of late September reminds me of all the students heading back to school. The Boston colleges are booming, I'm sure, with young people lugging mattresses and desks, chairs and rugs into dorms and crammed apartments. Henry always commented on the busy streets crowded with vans and the moving-in activities.

I don't miss any of that. As the third child of a career Air Force captain, I was used to moving in and out of places, hauling personal belongings inside and upstairs, but there was usually just one family at a time making this transition. At the city colleges it's a conglomeration of the masses, wildly ambitious to settle in, often with strangers. None of that appealed to me. My college years were spent at a small rural campus, where I knew most people well enough to say hello – it suited my subdued personality.

I think I'll pull on a sweater and sit in the sun for a bit. The surf seems calm today. I can barely hear the soft rush of salty foam embracing the shore.

Georgie seems content in his paddock munching on hay laced with pieces of carrot, celery, and peaches. He's a lovely fellow.

What an incredibly entrancing day this is, and yet my thoughts are partially with my daughter. I think of her adjustment in moving to a smaller home and to being alone. She has that little dog, but I wonder if he can fill the empty space left by Glenn's departure. Life is worth unfolding, even when unexpected change invades your space. Every now and then, the invasion is for the best, a plan you hadn't thought would work, and yet it does.

I've known the emptiness of life without Henry, and even though it's been eight years, I still think of asking him if he wants that second cup of coffee or tea, or if he wants pancakes for supper or chicken pot pie. I catered to his wishes. The man enjoyed eating, and I enjoyed the preparation. Though sometimes he'd cook, and that was always fine with me too. Now I consume whatever I feel like having, and sometimes that's homemade raspberry jam on good toast.

If I don't hear anything from Suzanna by later today, I'll call her this evening. I don't want to appear to be one more being who has learned to live without her. I have, but she doesn't need to hear or feel that from me. It's not her. It's what happens – people move on, change. It's her husband's desire for a different life, her children's wish to be independent, and her mother's wish to simply embrace life. All we can do is our best to transition. We all have to cope with change at one time or another.

* * *

In my call to Suzanna I discovered she's not been brooding over her predicament of living alone. She's been busy with the house, with Green Space, with Casper. In fact, she mentioned Casper several times. He sleeps with her, follows her from room to room, and she takes him for leisurely walks. Seems like she missed having a pet.

I was happy to hear her positive voice, a clear indication that she's transforming her life and making the best of change. She also mentioned someone named Joe, a Green Space enthusiast with draftsman abilities and his own construction company, who's been giving her a hand with some of the repairs. It sounds like she's found contentment.

Satisfied that she seems unperturbed, handling everything with a level head, I'll let her be the one to make the calls from now on. I was never on her trail as Henry was, and I have my doubts that she misses the interference as much as his friendship.

I remember looking out through our kitchen window in Jamaica Plain as the two of them played kickball. They looked like friends rather than father and daughter, and many times I wondered how it must feel to have that relationship with your child. I didn't know. I had introduced her to baking cookies, cupcakes, frying eggs without breaking the yolk, but she wasn't terribly impressed. Maybe it was me.

Every time I allow my mind to drift back to what

once was, I scold myself for feeling left out. My parents had a son, a daughter, then me. I'm sure I was an afterthought, or a mistake. Searching for a place in this universe was something I thought of but never actually did. As a child, I would spend time in Connecticut watching the narrow brook propel leaves to a pond not far away. I was pensive, aware that I might need to be enough for myself. Maybe no one else would ever care about who I was or where I was. I cared.

Well, it's after seven and starting to slide into night skies and a distant moon. I'll take some good treats to Georgie and tuck him in for the night. The air is excellent, dry and cool. I'll leave his screened window open. He's so much better here than in the big goat barn with all those frisky young males urging him to play. Georgie is over that I suppose, in the same way that I am over much of what I found entertaining in younger years.

It feels nice to have him settled in. I look forward to my own light supper and putting my feet up for a little TV, or maybe reading one of the books I bought this summer. Some might think I'm a lonely older woman, but I'm not in the least. I was lonelier as a child until I learned to fill my hours with my obligations first and with my pleasures after. As a teen, I was pretty certain I had no leverage within my family and friends, due to moving around so often. Relationships could be short-termed and sometimes scarce.

When there's no one around to question what you do

and when you do it, it feels freeing. Maybe Suzanna is grasping that perception as well. She was never the most popular girl as a child or teen, but that didn't seem to trouble her. Suzanna was smart, often reading or putting together a complex puzzle. She didn't make time for friends, and they made no time for her. I worried that she was lonely. I was acquainted with that feeling and didn't hope to share it with my daughter. Sometimes I feel it's strange that it was Henry who enjoyed the parent-child relationship to the point that I watched from the sidelines with a pang of envy.

Suzanna

I feel good about tackling the mountain of paperwork I've managed to sift through for Green Space. Their reports to the state, to the government, the requests for funds and for project acceptance are numerous. Maybe even overwhelming.

I've sorted everything into piles by category, but I'm running out of space on my counter. They have proposals for cleaner air sources, water projects encompassing multiple streams and rivers, flourishing gardens providing vegetables for those in need. Joe wrote one of the proposals, for an irrigation system to be installed by volunteer hands, so it can restore land to be filled with generous crops.

There's no end to their innovative ideas for making this world a healthier place. I'm impressed.

I love the completed work on my house. It's so small that sometimes I almost laugh at how I now live compared to what I once had. It's mine, it's big enough, and it's become a pretty little home.

Joe is suggesting that someday I might want to add a

room or two to accommodate visits from my children, my mother. It's not likely. My mother isn't fond of travel, especially on an airplane, and my kids, it's doubtful they'll ever come as a pair. I have a spare room that will do.

I've seen Joe's house. As a draftsman and contractor he's been very creative. He likes large windows and a post and beam atmosphere. I like his house, but I do wonder why a divorced man with one twenty-year-old son needs eight fairly large rooms. I suppose if you can afford it and you like it, why not?

I feel a tinge of joy when I think of Joe. He's not what I'd call handsome, but he's that rugged type seen on men's magazine covers with the scruffy beard, the firm body, intense eyes. But beyond the physical attributes, he's clever. He cares about the land and about all life being at its best.

He's different from anyone I've ever known. What a contrast to Glenn, who chose to pick up the phone over picking up a hammer, who owned little in clothing other than three-piece suits, crisp white shirts, and conservative ties. Joe probably wouldn't be caught dead in a three-piece suit.

I wish I could think of something that Glenn and I had shared a passion for. I haven't found it in myself to be angry with him. It must have been emotionally brutal to hide who he really was. I don't hate him and I don't miss him. He was never really there – even when he was.

Once I have Green Space's projects in good form, I may take another quick trip east. I enjoyed surprising my mother unaware last time. Of course, I got more than I'd bargained for. She equally surprised me with being off on a Connecticut excursion and keeping that goat a secret. She seemed startled – slightly intimidated – as if wondering if I might scold her. That never would have happened with my father. He'd have turned his wit to rage at my audacity – I can hear him saying that word – to show up unannounced and let myself in. And he would have been right. It was perhaps arrogant of me to just show up, to let myself into my mother's home. Nonetheless, I'm glad I found out about her. I'm glad, too, that she was willing to just let me be there. I intruded. She did not.

In her eighties now, she's more vulnerable, and that makes me worry. But I have the feeling that while she won't battle me on much, she wouldn't ever leave her home to move into an over fifty-five unit or into a facility where life is more guarded. I'd prefer she not be running all over the place, and the goat, he was a surprise. Maybe, instead, I'll call ahead and see if she's up for my company. I'd like to see that old goat again.

* * *

Well, that was an interesting phone call. Joe invited me to dinner at his favorite Mexican restaurant tomorrow night, around six. I was so surprised by the request for my company that I stuttered off an acceptance. Why not? I like Joe. He's a solidly sincere type, but I don't want him to think I'm one of those divorced women ready to fly. In fact, I'm not even officially divorced yet.

I shouldn't have accepted, but I did, and I'll go and be receptive and polite. I'll keep the conversation to a discussion concerning our upcoming projects. I won't be open to his visible charm. I'm absolutely not ready for another union. Not now, maybe never.

Is this what being married to Glenn has made of me? I suppose it has. I trusted the promise we made to one another long ago. I had children and put a home together. I've been the energy to the family without realizing I was running low on fuel. Why didn't I feel Glenn's absence even when he was at home?

Joe's invitation is going to mean a slight change in routine. I'll feed Casper and then take him for a walk around five or five-thirty, then I'll get dressed, but not elaborately. I'll keep it simple, dark slacks, a nice shirt, simple jewelry. I'll brush my hair and put it back, no romantic hair swinging against my shoulder blades. I'll be discreetly steady, as though the evening is more about business than social. My God, I'm totally overthinking this.

How many dates have I been on? In high school there were two boys who liked me, Jake and Daniel. They were nice and made passable prom companions. After one year in college and a trip back East for part of the summer, I ran into Jake who asked me out. I was busy and wanted to get back to California – I said no, politely.

After that, it was all about Glenn. He moved in on me so that I was flattered while feeling ushered into a relationship other girls envied. I felt special, but not in love.

I've missed so much, but I'm not so sure I care. Even if I had loved Glenn, he'd still have had these alternate desires, and then what? I'd be sitting here with a broken heart. Instead, I feel nothing. Maybe not nothing, but very little.

With Casper nestled at my side, I feel his warmth, probably more than I've known in my entire life. In all fairness, my cat was comforting as well, glad to have my lap while I feasted on a good book. It's really quite wonderful to have a pet again. It's good to be loved.

Before I turn in for the night, I'll have a look in my closet. I know I'll wear my dark gray slacks, but which blouse? I have that nice amethyst silk with long sleeves, and I could wear that with my denim blazer, keeping it casual. Or I could wear my black shirt, the soft rayon with the tiny silver buttons.

The idea that I was feeling anxious about having accepted Joe's offer makes me smile. The more I think about it, the more I'm looking forward to our time together. I can't refer to it as a date though. Not yet.

Sadearah

Every single day, cloudy or bright, is a blessing. I've always treasured climbing into a warm bed at night and then opening my eyes to a new day. I've loved seeing a fresh snow fall, the leaves turning to paint-box displays, rain making everything new again, and sun stretching across the trees creating magical shadows. Every shining moment has been worth making it through the losses, the questions and doubts.

I wondered what all the talk was from my sister when she was on her death bed. I stayed at her place for three days, holding her hand, giving her sips of water while the hospice nurse took brief breaks. Esther murmured some strange things those last hours, words I could not comprehend. They made no sense at the time. Now I wonder what she was trying to tell me. Those two years she lived away, out by a lake in Wisconsin, her life was a mystery. I remember that my mother insisted she take a job out there. I didn't want Esther to go. I was somewhat entranced by her beauty, always seeking to understand what I was missing. Was I underrated? I didn't want to be her, or anything like her, yet I was drawn to what I didn't hope to be.

She went away as my mother told her to and returned seeming different. Maturity had set in, or maybe it was the reaction from divorcing Tom. Possibly it was all settling at my sister's feet and the solemnity of it all had made her quiet. I failed to understand the transformation.

On her death bed, she said Clayton several times. I'd never heard that name before anywhere. I tried to ask her who that was, but she would just smile in her sleep and say the word *baby*, then *beautiful baby*, then *Clayton*. I had no one who could tell me who Clayton was. Had my mother sent my sister away to have a child born from an affair? Or, worse, from the husband who had caused the end of an unborn two years before? It made sense. My mother would do that, but then where was this Clayton? Had Esther given birth to a little boy and left him to be raised in Wisconsin?

I shuddered as I held my sister's fragile hand, wondering what terrible nightmares she must have suffered for her beauty. Tom was a horror. He'd hurt her in many ways, and other boys and men had taken turns as well. My mother would execute the orders and yes, I could see her sending Esther away to conceal a pregnancy and birth. If a child was conceived, he'd be older than Suzanna, perhaps fifty-eight or nine. I'll never know.

I cannot understand my mother participating in a

delusion that her beautiful daughter was away for professional purposes. And I wonder if having a grandchild more than a thousand miles away, one she would never see or know, might have bothered her. A farm girl with highbrow standards might not have given a thought or name to a baby born at an inconvenient time. Perhaps it's best I don't know, but the more I give thought to those last days Esther had in the comfort of her own bed, the more I think that Clayton was part of us and I wonder where he might be.

It seems that the qualities some families are made of contain hidden, dark secrets. But who are they protecting? It bothers me to think, as much as my mother was nasty to me, that she would have done something like that, mental torture in so many ways, to her own flesh and blood. Having lived in that conflicted environment, I cannot doubt that acts and deeds might have been concealed. So determined, my mother was the force behind us all. I never understood her. I never will. And I strive to be everything she was not.

I willingly caress all that I can see and do at this time in my life. I was never free before now, growing up in military life, then off to college, then to marriage. I feel like I was under someone's thumb for endless years, and here I am, in this small house on a massive stretch of beach enjoying independence with a gray goat. I can smile and feel not the slightest tinge of guilt. I'll be damned if anyone, and certainly not Suzanna, will ever have their thumb on me again.

Accepting that there is little or nothing I can do about my past, or the remnants of memories concerning my family, I plan to live each day cherishing the good moments, and I'll figure out as I go along how to deal with difficulties such as my daughter. I have the distinct feeling that she's going to try to maneuver my life so that it suits her more than it suits me. That's not going to happen. I make my own choices.

Maybe I give more time to thought than I should. Not that it harms anyone else, but it causes me to question what I might have done alternatively to change sorrows within my family. Observing a strict yet fair father, an insistent and maybe not fair mother, a brother who seemed anxious to escape, and a sister who was too pretty to be taken seriously, who – or maybe the better question is what was I to them? Underrated, unwanted. But that was more on them than me. I managed to stay out of the way most of the time. That night I defended Esther, when my mother slapped me with that awful name, I learned to keep my thoughts to myself, even more than I ever had before.

Perhaps that's why I adapted so easily to what Henry expected of me. He liked my quick answers, my quick thinking brain, my free thoughts delivered with a soft voice and often a smile. I liked that he liked me. I wasn't sure anyone else ever had. And so I followed his wish that we become one, and then since it seemed important for him to make the majority of decisions, I became agreeable. Now I wish I had shown a bit of resistance. I had opinions, but I had been trained young to believe that what I felt was not significant. How awful.

The next segment of my journey is to keep Suzanna at bay. While I feel for her present difficulties and changes she's met, I will not accept her executing what and when I eat, sleep, or where I live. This is it for me, and I'm prepared to fight.

She's probably quite proud of herself to have caught me by showing up here unannounced, finding me gone away and having acquired a goat. She seemed a bit haughty about discovering my secrets. But I don't answer to her. Inside, I was almost laughing, realizing that I'd surprised her, that bright woman I'd raised. She saw that there's more to me than a submissive wife and mother. We are flesh and blood, yet what is both sad and interesting is that there's little grace in that knowledge.

Suzanna

It feels good to be home. My evening with Joe was casual. Our conversation led him to tell me how his divorce nearly crippled him emotionally when it first occurred. I felt sorry for him, but I don't understand grieving for someone who wants to erase a relationship. I am definitely not doing that. Glenn's life was Glenn's life, not mine. It had been his secret. My only fault is that I was living with a blindfold securely fastened. I keep asking myself what I failed to see. But, then again, I wasn't looking. I was content, or believed I was. Now I know differently.

Entering my own little home is a respite. And I liked being out with Joe. He's different from other men I've known – gentle where my father had been stern, giving with his sentiments which Glenn was not. And I appreciate that he didn't push for more than friendship, getting to know one another. Why rush?

All I do know is that I don't want any baggage. My own or someone else's. There are better things to do than spend evenings and days dwelling on failure. I'm done with being worried about what I should have noticed or done differently. Now is a time for looking forward to being integral to someone or something. But, for now, I don't need to worry about anyone but Casper and me. My children are capable people who don't need me. My mother seems okay when I call to check in, but I worry about her. And if the need arises, though she will likely resist, if she becomes irrational or starts falling, I may need to step in and decide her future.

I'll go out there again soon. It was fun to surprise her last time, not announcing my arrival. It makes me mad though that she hides aspects of her life from me. I wonder what else she isn't telling me, situations that might be uncomfortable for both of us. It would be so much easier for me, and she would be so much better off out here in a nice facility where I could oversee her care and stop in every now and then to observe her progress.

I'm so glad I didn't have to do that with Dad. He would have resisted. I don't think my mother has ever thought to impede anyone or anything. It amazes me sometimes when I think of all she accomplished so quietly. And as much as I'd like to think she'd do well in a place where all she had to do was watch TV and read books, it would certainly make life easier for me if I didn't have to keep flying back east, something tells me she wouldn't willingly leave her cottage or her goat. There's either more to her than I've ever known or she's not stable. I just haven't figured out which yet.

If only she could be more like Casper. This little dog

is obedient and companionable. Had he not come with the house, I'm sure I would have found a cat to live with, but Casper gets me motivated to take a walk at least once each day. It's good for both of us, emotionally and physically. We're lucky to have found one another.

It makes me wonder about my mother and that goat of hers. Who in the world gets a goat for a pet and lives with it on a beach at Cape Cod? My father would have absolutely said no to that decision. He liked animals okay, but a farm animal? No, I don't think so. That's where he'd have drawn the line. And while I certainly have no plans to get a goat, I have to admit that he was pretty sweet.

Relaxing each evening with a glass of wine is new to me. I keep questioning how I once lived, so orderly. Up at the crack of dawn, off to work at the office where little lives were swiped from bad parenting to strange homes, then back to a great but empty house. In my new world I have less to take care of, the freedom of loving my work with Green Space, and the pure luxury of doing absolutely nothing if I choose. Other than caring for Casper, of course. I never thought this would be my destination, simplicity in living small with a grateful little dog. It's hard for me to accept that I am actually happier now than I ever was before. Beneath the thumb of my father and then my husband, I was well-trained.

I can't help but follow my thoughts as they wander to Kira and to Jordan. Neither Glenn nor I tried to manipulate our children. They were bright kids with good grades, exceptionally normal from my point of view. Jordan's music had been a gift to him as well as to us. It made everyone happy. Kira had managing aspects which sometimes made us laugh – she liked telling Jordan what to wear. And now that I think of it, it might have been that she was the one of us who saw that what he chose to wear was revealing. I remember a lavender colored shirt he seemed to choose often, and a t-shirt that was decorated in rainbows. I looked at his casual apparel as being playful, in tune with his music. Kira may have been more aware about the selected garments, protective of her brother's reputation – not to mention hers, and tried to direct him toward something more masculine. Now I wonder if that's why they live so far apart, unable to find comfortable agreement in their diverse lives.

Had Glenn and I been oblivious parents? Shouldn't we have noticed that our son was living in contrast to us? Perhaps the marriage was not the only failure. Were we so engrossed in our own careers that we didn't notice? And did we not see that our daughter was moving away from us emotionally? Would that have compelled her to relocate to city life? It doesn't come easy, this parenting.

I wonder what my children would think, if they'd even care, that another man has sought my company. It doesn't matter though. If Joe asks me out again, which he alluded to, I may find a reason not to accept. Not that I don't find him interesting or that I wouldn't want to see him socially again, but in my own conflicted life, I feel the immediate need for complacency rather than conversations about what fell apart in his life, or mine. Focusing on failures is exhausting.

Sadearah

On a crisp evening like this, I am reminded that October is my favorite month. This is the season of color, pumpkins, apples, leaves, and summer's bounty of beautiful blooms, all gathered to create a great show before November slows the process and winter waits to be invited in. Every season has its purpose. I'll enjoy a good wood fire when the snowflakes fly, and then embrace the holidays. The best is on the way.

I wonder what Suzanna will do this Thanksgiving. She invited Henry and me one year, but Henry, who didn't like those plane trips and who favored New England for Thanksgiving, said thank you but no. I was glad, although I would have gone at least that once. She never extended the invitation again.

We haven't had a holiday with Suzanna since she married. Henry and I did fine on our own, often inviting friends from our Jamaica Plain neighborhood in for a festive drink and little treats. I made my stuffed mushrooms and cranberry-laced cornbread. I served one-inch squares of rich brownies and star-shaped sugar cookies. Nothing was left by the time the last visitor went home – everyone opted to take a few treats with them. Henry and I always looked at the empty plates and laughed.

Now that I live more simply here on the Cape, I don't invite anyone in. Most of my neighbors are here only in summer, and those that are here year round are not nearby or, like Kate, are busy with their own lives. I don't miss living in a tightly arranged neighborhood – what I have now is much better. And I don't miss cleaning up after the big gatherings. But, oh, how I do love the holiday season.

I look forward to putting up a little tree sprinkled with tiny lights and a few old ornaments. I'll put my sea shell collection around the bottom as usual. I can't wait. This year I'll bring Georgie inside on Christmas Eve. Heck, I'll bring him inside any time I want to. If it gets cold, why should he quiver with chilled air when he would be just fine on a rug in my kitchen? This is going to be one of the most fun holiday seasons I've ever known.

I'll make a scarf and hat for Georgie so he won't be too cold on our walks. I have no presents to buy. I'll send a check to Kira, to Jordan, and to Suzanna. They have their own taste, no thanks or comments about what I've purchased in the past. In fact, Suzanna told me she took something back I'd bought her five or six years ago. It wasn't her style or color. At the same time, I've given away things she gave to me. We just don't know each other anymore. Maybe we never did. How did I manage to do anything right? I suppose I'm not certain that I ever did, until now.

Maybe it wasn't perfect, but it was certainly more civil when I was growing up. If someone gave you a gift, you thanked them and said you loved it. It wasn't honest, but there's an old adage which declares that truth hurts.

Perhaps I'll venture off to Connecticut one more time before winter sets in. The snows in the Berkshires can be hazardous though, so I should go soon. I'll give Stephen a call to see if we can meet for a bite. He's such a pleasant young man. I imagine he must have been a wonderful son. At the same time, neither of us has mentioned much about family. Maybe I'll take some of my little brownies to him. I can package them up with a length of red ribbon and sign the card from Georgie and me. And I'll draw a little goat on the tag.

Whimsical art was something I always added to Christmases past. Those days hold fond memories. I loved seeing what Douglas and Esther opened from under the tree. Their gifts seemed grown up to me, intricate sets to build cars and cabins for Doug, glamorous hair barrettes and pretty dresses for Esther. For me it was usually a thick package of crayons, coloring books, and a tin of watercolor paints. Once in a while there would be a teddy bear or a little doll, and I always received new socks.

I can't remember what my father and mother gave to one another. Henry and I always exchanged gifts.

Nothing extravagant, but thoughtful. The year before he died I bought him a nice warm navy blue hat with a wide brim to catch the snow. He loved it and wore it often. I could, come to think of it, give it to Georgie instead of knitting a new one. It would look very dapper on him, and if Henry has grown a sense of humor in Heaven, he'll smile.

My last Christmas gift from Henry, who passed in March of that year, was a delicate pink silk scarf, which I keep fastened to my bed post. I say a silent goodnight to my partner of forty-seven years with my eyes on that ethereal fabric, remembering how cheerful that color was in the depth of winter. I have good memories, yet there are times when I recall wondering how much I mattered. I don't think it was my imagination that both as a child and as a wife and mother, I was always the third wheel.

It's all gone now, and maybe it would be best if I could stop it from circling in my thoughts. I don't know how to forget. What I know is how to survive. I've managed to find a place in this world where I smile, I enjoy, I dig and delve into what interests me, like the goat farm and my Georgie.

How amused Henry would be to think I wanted a goat. He'd have said no of course, but here I am with a charming companion with whom I will share the holidays. I'll make Georgie some of my good cornbread, just a little to go with his feed. And on both Thanksgiving and Christmas morning, I will toast to

Henry with a good cup of coffee before preparing a celebratory meal. Not necessarily the traditional fare, but whatever we feel like having. Maybe French toast with real maple syrup or corn fritters swimming in butter. It will be fun to indulge, and I can share a bit with Georgie – a delightful taste and a bundle of love.

I wonder if Suzanna shares food from her plate with Casper. I haven't heard from her in nearly a week now. I hope that means she's enjoying her new home and position with Green Space. Perhaps I know what I should do for her this Christmas – make a nice donation in her name to that very industrious organization. Sending my daughter money is like sending her a desert plant – she has all she needs. The donation would speak to her interest. Dare I include a pretty scarf or pair of gloves? Maybe not. I'll have to think about that. It just feels like I can't do anything quite right as far as she's concerned.

How strange it is that the flesh that comes from your body becomes your critic rather than a sweet attachment. I know it's not the same for everyone, but for my mother, and for me, it seems we gave birth to children who grew up independent of us. Suzanna has never spoken to me about what she thought of me as a parent, but it seemed evident that she didn't like me much. It was Henry, always Henry, who had her respect.

I think about when I am no more. I don't expect or want Suzanna to weep at my passing, but I do hope she turns me to my grave knowing that I cared. I always

132

cared.

That's why I feel the need to go to Connecticut. Even though my grandparents never gave me so much as a card, there I felt loved, cared about, like I belonged. I cannot wait to go back. I'll drive there before Thanksgiving and stay overnight again. Three hours of driving each way is getting tiresome for me, but an overnight at least allows me to rest if not actually sleep.

And hopefully I'll enjoy a little visit with Stephen. If he's available, I will surely bake those little brownies for him. I've noticed he likes a sweet after lunch. If he was just closer, I could make a nice dinner for Thanksgiving and invite him to join Georgie and me.

He knows I have a pet goat and laughed as he said that he must be a wonderful "kid," except that Georgie is not in his youth. Nevertheless, we were in agreement and enjoyed the merriment as I told of how I came to decide on adopting. It feels genuinely fine not to be criticized for a decision I've made.

If I don't have a call from Suzanna in the next few days, maybe I'll call Kira. Certainly she and her mother must talk often and she'd tell me if anything was amiss with my daughter.

Kira would probably be surprised to get a call from me. How strange that blood families often disengage. I would have loved a shared closeness with my child and my grandchildren, but they knew where I was, they had my phone number. The times I called each of them I was met with politeness but a sense of being kind of a pest.

After a few calls to each one, I stopped. If I make the call to Kira, I'll keep it short. After all, we're practically strangers. Here she is living just a few short hours away and she never even considers a visit. And if she did, I don't think either of us would know what to say to the other.

Suzanna

I just lied to Joe about what I was doing this weekend. He wanted to know if I liked to hike and suggested we could take a picnic and explore a local trail. I do like him, he's a wonderful asset to Green Space, but he has these heavy weights attached to his heart. I just can't compete with that right now.

I suppose I should call my mother. I'm always half afraid that we'll have nothing to say to one another or that I'll say the wrong thing. Talking to her just isn't easy – it's hard to get an actual answer out of her. I certainly can't ask if she's lonely or if she needs anything in particular from me. How can I help her when she's on the other side of the country? It would be so much easier if she just sold that house and moved here. But something tells me that there's stubbornness in her quiet, that I wouldn't get anywhere suggesting she move. I do worry about her, whether she's keeping up with the bills and buying groceries. There wasn't a whole lot in the fridge when I went last time. Then again, there's not much in my fridge now. When there's only one person to provide for, not much is needed. I recall often of how organized my dad was, how he dealt with just about everything. It makes me think that my mother must be a bit lost without his direction. How could she be anything but depressed and lonely without his constant presence?

Glenn wasn't around enough to be as prominent in our lives, but still, like Dad, he wanted what he wanted. I think I let him get away with having his will too often. I always asked what he wanted for dinner – he never once asked me. Not about dinner or the evening or the weekend. But now I can do as I please.

This weekend I'll pop Casper into the car and drive north. I think the change will be nice and I'll avoid being here where Joe could drive by and see my car. I've lied to him, so now I need to make it work. I'm kind of annoyed with myself for not just telling him the truth, that I need more time before I consider the dating scene. Then again, I'm not sure if I can call it dating. That might not be his intent. Maybe he just longs to have a shoulder to cry on. But I'm not looking to have a soggy shoulder.

Before my weekend journey, I should call my mother, make sure she has my cell number handy in case there's an emergency. It would have been so much easier had Dad been the one left. He'd probably have stayed in the Jamaica Plain house or he'd have moved out here with me. Mother is the difficult, hard to read one.

Kira and Jordan will never have this dilemma when I

reach my golden years. I'm unmistakably independent. No one will ever have to worry about me. My mother is a different tale. She's always been told what to do and when to do it. I'm not sure she'd have managed to survive without Dad's and my guidance. Yet there she is, harboring an old goat in my father's summer shed on the Cape.

I often wonder how she convinced Dad to spend summers there. She had all sorts of social involvements in the city, yet she preferred the desolate stretches of beach, the solitary existence. Dad must be rolling in his grave at her decision to sell the house and move to the cottage. Life is unpredictably strange.

Dad, oddly so, had very few social connections. He went to work, came home, and settled in for a quiet evening with a good meal under his belt. He was complete in who he was, not needing to search for outside associations.

I've always considered myself to be more like my Dad. I've formed a life and haven't felt the pull toward others. I do like the Green Space folks, but it's more Green Space and its positive impact on the globe that interests me.

* * *

This little bed and breakfast is perfect for tonight. They are fine with Casper, and in fact have two little dogs themselves. The room is comfortable, the bathroom private, and the view from a bay window is beautiful. The hills in the distance make me feel a pang

137

of guilt for lying to Joe – he had plans for us to hike this sort of area. Maybe some day. I don't know.

Having been tied to someone for thirty years, it feels both freeing and slightly terrifying to be on my own. I've never been on my own before. I like being able to come and go as I please without explanations to anyone else, but I also feel abandoned. I suppose in time I'll adjust to this, but for now, I need to move on. If only I was certain about *how* to move on, and *where* to move onto.

I've wondered a few times lately if I would have felt the same way if Glenn, like my father, had died. This divorce is about Glenn choosing another life. This is about leaving me behind, in spite of rearing two children together. How did this happen?

I wish I had a confidante – I really have no one with whom I could have a discussion about what fails and why. Some might suggest I talk to my mother, but she's never seemed emotionally available. Well, to be honest with myself, I've never thought I needed her. Part of this gloom and doom is probably on me. I don't think so, but my opinions at the moment might not be up to the issue.

I'll take my little ghost dog and have a walk, then I'll find some dinner he and I can share. I'm tired, and I just want to settle in this room where I can watch TV with Casper.

Sadearah

Suzanna's calls assure me that she's fine, yet I think she can be quite insulting. The questions she asks me, as if I'm a child. Did you do this? Did you do that? Do you still have that goat? I want to tell her to mind her own business, to mend her own life, and that I am doing splendidly. I listen and say little. My defense is to reply to her with dignity and calm. I would gain nothing at all by telling her off, except, a little satisfaction.

It would be so pleasant to think of planning a holiday gathering with my child and my grandchildren, but the fact remains they have their own lives and are not at all interested in spending time with an elderly relative. Kira and Jordan probably don't even know about Georgie, and that's fine. They'd more than likely be in agreement with their mother, that the advanced years have taken me to a place they choose not to visit.

As a child, whenever I could have a summer break from military life and visit with my grandparents on the farm, I felt I was in absolute Heaven. I loved the meadows and hills surrounding their place, but I also loved listening to them, following them around, learning to plant flowers and churn butter. It seemed that every moment of their days mattered. There was never contemplation for what to do next.

They didn't have an abundance of money. I was never given a gift of any kind from them. Their gift was allowing me into their world.

I remember Doug going there for a week or two of our summer vacations, but I don't recall Esther ever being there at all. There were very few boys and lots of chores. The routine would not have been anything Esther would have cared for. She missed so much. She chose to be noticed for her physical attributes and not for her mind. I know she had a strong ability to learn, at times she could be perceptive. As her younger sister though, I couldn't have admired her just because she was beautiful. She wasn't a piece of art.

Suzanna is so like her in looks. The resemblance stops there as my daughter is more organized, a business-oriented woman, where Esther allowed others to take care of her. Too often that care resulted in disappointment and emotional injury.

I wish I had the opportunity to revisit my sister's teen years and say to her the things I thought, that she was finding solace in all the stupid, horrible people who simply wanted her on their arms as a decoration. Why did she need that? I could be wrong, yet I feel her life was wasted. No surviving marriage out of two, and no children. And then I continue to wonder about that name

Clayton.

I always feel I go backward in time when I've talked to Suzanna. Her words remind me of what I may have overlooked in my youth, and I wonder what I should have done instead of what I did. Henry was a factor in my decision for the future. I have no idea why he decided to pursue me. If he did *settle* for me as his parents seemed to think, then I wish he'd left me alone instead. I am better and more deserving than being someone's second best. Maybe, though, his parents were wrong. He never did anything that led me to believe he cared for me less than he should.

Every time I think of Henry, there's an instinct to glance over at his desk. That desk was his prized possession. I watched him sit there every single night without fail, checking his calendar, paying a bill, thumbing through the register to make certain he'd forgotten nothing. It was part of his day, if even for just a few moments.

When I think back about how we were as a young couple, and then grew to mingle one another's likes and dreams, we had a decent marriage. It was, in spite of what I overheard from his mother, a compatible relationship. But did I love him? And did he love me? Or did we just settle for each other because that was what was expected of us? I don't know why I torment myself with these questions. It's over and done with, and what I have left is that desk, my pink scarf, and many memories of a life well lived together. I definitely could have done worse. I could have been deceived then abandoned like my poor daughter.

In our conversation this evening, Suzanna never once mentioned Glenn. It's like he was never part of her life, or she part of his. The few times they came east to visit us, I found him agreeable but not warm. I felt he almost feared being around us, and now I wonder if he was awkward about who he was. Did he think we might notice something different about him?

When Suzanna told me about Glenn's revelation, I said nothing. My daughter needed to reveal the truth. She didn't need my input. I listened to her words and heard her bewilderment. It would have surprised me had she cried. She was stoic until her voice cracked. At that moment, I hesitated then told her I was sorry. Henry would have said much more.

Now she's out there alone with the fires and earthquakes. I can't think that she'd ever give California up and return to the East. She's stubborn, and she has Green Space now to occupy her. She'll be efficient for them. The environmental concerns have always been an interest of hers and of mine. I think it's the one subject we agree on – we both feel an urgency to protect our planet. I'm proud of her for that.

I remember when she was in the tenth grade and there were two options on a Saturday involving her school. The first was a meeting to plan for a dance, a sophomore hop. The second was a group of kids, led by the earth science teacher, being taken to a twisting road in town where an accumulation of trash had been scattered by careless drivers. It was Suzanna's choice to pick up trash. Neither Henry nor I tried to influence her to do one over the other. Henry said very little, but I know he was proud. I was deeply moved by her decision. She's a good girl, a worthwhile person, but I do wish she felt a little more endearment for her family. Of course, that would be me at this point, and my hopes are muffled. I'm not even sure I'd know what to do if she decided to come live out here. Either she'd be breathing down my neck, second guessing every decision I make, and trying to control me or she'd be just as distant emotionally as she is now. What good would it do? It's not like she'd happily come over regularly for tea and a sweet.

It strikes me as funny that she called to make sure I have her cell number in case there's an *emergency* while she's away for the weekend. So now that she's called and won't call again for a week or so, I am free to head out to Connecticut. I'll see the foliage and I'll cherish my moments by the farm. I'll call Stephen to see what his schedule looks like then make my plans based on his availability. The whole week ahead is supposed to be beautiful. And even if he isn't going to have time, I'll go anyway.

I'll pack a change of clothes and leave Georgie with plenty of feed and extra hay all around him to keep him warm. People think that because an animal is an outdoor creature, living in a barn out of the weather, that they are fine with the cold. I've seen the little ones at the local farm shivering in the chilled air. Their coats aren't that thick – surely they prefer a warm bed at night.

* * *

My call to Stephen was sweet. He's the nicest man I think I've ever known. He and I will meet for lunch tomorrow at the café where we first met. I'll pack tonight and leave in the morning around seven. That will put me near the farm by ten-thirty to eleven with plenty of time to connect with Stephen.

Goodness, with Thanksgiving just a couple of weeks away, I'm late in going. I'll make those little chocolate brownies tonight after I get Georgie tucked in. I know Stephen will enjoy them.

From here to the Mass Pike will be a bit more than an hour. After a long length on the Pike I'll be heading toward Hartford and the network of roads that take me northwest through to Winderlee and the farm. From there the café is just two or three miles. This is going to be a treat, something to joyfully remember through the cold winter months ahead.

* * *

What a nice lunch Stephen and I shared.

The booth where we were seated in the café was my favorite, right by a large window that overlooks a small pond. Stephen and I ordered our lunch then sat watching the mallards and Canada Geese pecking at the dried grass, seeming content with their own fare.

We chatted about what we had been up to the last few months and what we were doing for the holidays. His

144

family had asked him to be with them for Thanksgiving on Long Island. He was reluctant to go, but agreed. I revealed that I was making a meal to share with my goat and that I would then put up my little Christmas tree. Stephen smiled and said he might just do the same when he was back from Long Island.

We talked about Christmas and I remembered to fish out of my large purse the little package of brownies. He was pleased and sampled one before our lunch was served. He said they were the best he'd ever had.

He asked if I'd see Suzanna for Christmas, and I told him that I didn't think so as she generally stays in California. I didn't mention that she was going through a divorce and that her children live a distance away. When he asked what I would do, I told him that I'll make dinner again for Georgie and me and we'll have a leisurely time admiring the tree.

Stephen had smiled and asked, "Georgie will be with you looking at the tree?"

"Yes. Last year was his first winter with me and I had several nights when I brought him inside to the kitchen. I have a rug by the sink and I put down an extra blanket or two. He loves it. He's a very good boy."

Stephen laughed again. "By the way you treat him, he *should* be a very good boy."

Our lunch was served and we talked about what we'd been doing and what the future held. Stephen had told me before that he'd been married soon after college, just like Suzanna. He and his wife had a son, Michael, and when Michael was six, his marriage had dissolved.

He had tried to make a living with his art, which from photos he'd shown me, were exquisite, bright, beautiful paintings of country roads and cabins by a lake. His wife had called it his hobby. His father had told him to get a real job. At that point, he moved toward Winderlee where he became an auditor for a private banking system, working often from home. He found time to paint in his evening hours, and sometimes during the day when the light came into his place too perfect to ignore.

I could envision this sweet man, not traditionally handsome, but appealing head to toe, embracing his gift. I'm sure he dealt with his father's lack of faith and his wife, who considered Stephen's talent to be a diversion, with a definite measure of charm. I can't imagine him doing anything else. It must have been discouraging as well as disheartening. Had this been my son, I'd have enjoyed every moment of his creativity. I'd have supported his spirit. Parents are, however, just humans, and sometimes they say or do the wrong thing. Maybe that's why with Suzanna I tend to keep my thoughts to myself. You can't say something you'll regret if you're quiet. But I don't need to worry about that with Stephen. We connect.

Our luncheon was perfect, good food and good conversation. Every time we meet I find I like him more. A fleeting thought of him with my Suzanna drifted through my mind, but I wondered how supportive she

146

would be of his artistic skills.

When we parted, I drove back to the farm, parked near to my grandfather's old barn, then walked past the bow-roofed house and lingered for a moment looking at the window on the second floor. That window was in the bedroom I occupied, with pale pink wallpaper and white chrysanthemums as the prominent design. It was beautiful, a sunny place arranged with three twin-sized beds so that grandchildren could sleep there together. Most often I had the room to myself as Doug would sleep in the spacious attic and Esther stayed with mother and dad wherever they were stationed. She was always about the boys, and there were plenty at every military base.

I relish seeing the old place again, along with the last of the brilliant foliage, burnt umber slicing through the trees, softening the blaze of orange and red leaves. Every time I'm there I ask myself the same question, why not buy a small place in Winderlee instead of living at the Cape? The answer is always the same. The loneliness for those who once occupied this land is strong. I could not remain there day after day without them. A visit is all I can bear.

Each time I return home after two days away I feel both weary and exhilarated. The recollection of my journey is always a joy for days and weeks that follow. I never think it's my last time there, although someday it will be. The weariness I feel is a good feeling, a time to reflect in my comfortable old chair, my feet up with a good cup of coffee in hand.

Over and over my thoughts will revisit the farm, the conversation with Stephen, and the rolling hills. It will be nice, though, to be home with Georgie. He'll be happy to see me, and I know he'll enjoy the apples I bring him from Connecticut.

I wonder what Suzanna will do for Thanksgiving. Maybe she'll go to New York and spend a few days with Kira. She could take in the festivities of the parade and the stores being embellished for Christmas. I always wanted to go there for the parade, or for New Year's Eve when Times Square is filled to capacity with human spirit. Henry was avidly against such wishes. Strange that a person who so embraced the city objected to crowds. I took pleasure in watching the parade and celebrations on TV, and at this point in my life, that's enough. It feels very sensible to be an octogenarian who accepts the inevitable, less ability to do what is intended for the young. It's okay. It's normal.

Last year I made myself a nice meal and shared parts of it with Georgie. I had just adopted him and the look in his eyes when he tasted mashed potato and corn bread was priceless. I feel certain he thought it was better than munching on balsam and pine. This year he will enjoy the same.

Other than that, the holiday had been quiet. I had thought there might be a call from my daughter or someone in my family. I heard nothing, as though I had been forgotten. How have I come to expect that? In a way, it might seem sad to some, but for me, it's what I'm accustomed to. I was last to be considered in my family, and now my own child handles me in the same way – an afterthought at best. I suppose I could protest, demand some attention. But who am I to force her into something that isn't what she wants? Who would I have been to alter her path to contentment and fulfillment? I was enough for myself growing up. I'm still okay. In fact, I'm *very* okay. It's time to move on.

* * *

Driving home, thinking of my life, I was sort of ghostly. While isolating, it could be fun. Since no one ever really noticed me, I was free to do as I wished, just as I did at the farm, exploring meadows, visiting the cows, talking to the reddish salamanders at the brook. I had a heck of a good time, always taking in the oddities and pure beauty of nature. I loved looking at the tree trunk forms and the twisted limbs reaching out for sun and rain. I sketched them when I remembered to take a pad and pencil with me, and if I didn't have one handy, I sketched what I could remember when I was back at my grandparents' home. I could be wrong, but I think I've had an exemplary life.

This year if I don't hear from Suzanna by Thanksgiving, I'll be brave and make the call. I am, after all, her mother, and Henry would have called her at seven in the morning her time, just to get her going and to see what she intended to serve with the turkey.

For me, the turkey could have been omitted. I never

liked seeing an entire carcass on the table, as if there was zero respect for the animal's life. I liked the butternut squash, the stuffing, and the buttery mashed potato. But no, Henry was an expert at cooking the turkey, basting the turkey, then slicing it neatly. I watched him many times, amused at his surgical techniques. He liked perfection and lived to demonstrate that asset many times.

Yes, if I don't hear from Suzanna by mid-day on Thanksgiving, I'll make the call.

Suzanna

My days fade into one another, dissolving my emotions while keeping my sanity on track. I called Kira about Thanksgiving, and she's committed to her boyfriend's family. I asked if I could stay at her apartment while she was in White Plains for that day, but she said it would not be a good time for her to have a guest. A guest. Am I not more than a guest to my daughter?

I didn't argue the point. I got off the phone as quickly as possible. I don't think she has ever been aware of me shedding a tear, and I'm not going to start now.

I waited several hours before getting up the nerve to call Jordan. His plans are signed and sealed. He is going to Michael's family in Seattle for four days over Thanksgiving. Neither of my children asked what my plans include. Nothing, they include nothing.

I briefly considered visiting my mother, but I've decided against it. What will she think, knowing no one in my family wants to be with me? And if she said no too, I'm not sure I could bear the rejection. No, it's better to not ask for an invitation.

As though reading my mind, the phone rings. Surprisingly, I am actually happy to report that I am being included by someone – Joe. He's invited his sister and her husband, along with a few people from Green Space, to enjoy a Thanksgiving feast. I've offered to bring a couple of desserts, an apple pie and a lemon chiffon cake. He graciously accepted.

The idea of this feels right to me. I won't be spending time alone with Joe, which at this point would be awkward, and I'll have the opportunity to mingle with others.

I'll call my mother that morning and see what she's doing. She's probably inviting people in as she did for several years in Jamaica Plain. Now if this was my father, I'd be concerned about him being alone. But not my mother. She's a different type. I'm not sure she even likes the holidays, any of them.

I wonder what Glenn will be doing for Thanksgiving. Will he even celebrate? He'll no doubt be in Japan. Is he alone or has he moved on to someone else? I don't even know if he left me to be with another or just so he could live his own life, unencumbered. We didn't talk about it. Do thoughts of guilt and what ifs run through his mind as well?

While he wasn't one to cook very often, I think of him in years past, preparing the turkey, basting it every couple of hours, making a chestnut stuffing. I feel the pang for those times when everything seemed so normal. What I have these days is exactly the opposite.

Everything is new to me, and I'm not sure I'm handling it well.

There will be no leftovers for the next day, not that I care so much, except for the tradition involving making the open-faced sandwiches drenched in gravy. I recall us enjoying those leftovers as much or more than the actual dinner.

I wonder when I think of these past memories when it will all stop. I want it to stop, and yet I want to remember. That was part of my life, a time when we were all together if even for a day or two. Where did everything go? Why did it go? Glenn is off on a new escapade, boldly living in a new country. My children are living in states far removed from where they lived until college and work opportunities. I'm the only one left here, and the only one of the four of us who was not born to California. What is the matter with this scenario?

I'm so glad I won't be spending the holiday alone.

* * *

I tried calling my mother and there was no answer. When I spoke with her yesterday, the conversation seemed to go fairly well. I thought I'd call her and drop a hint that I might take another journey there soon. Maybe it's best I keep that to myself and just show up again on her doorstep. Who knows? She might have accumulated another goat she's not telling me about.

In the meanwhile, I'll take Casper for a drive and then take my time meandering toward home. Joe's unexpectedly stopped by a couple of times on his way home from work. I'd just as soon not be around when he happens by. I'm not happy with going out of my way to avoid him, but I feel the need to keep him at arm's length, at least for now. My father would probably have agreed with me. He'd tell me not to rush into another relationship so soon after parting with my husband.

I need a coffee. I'll grab my purse, put Casper on his lead, and we'll head out for a short ride – maybe take a little walk – then return to our own little home. Filled with both old and new chairs, dishes, cups, and photographs, it's comfortable. There's a familiarity about my environment, my fresh new life. It's as if this is what my soul's been searching for.

* * *

It's incredibly beautiful here in the hills, but I'm tired of letting everyone else claim my life. Now that I've taken control of my home, my happiness, it's time to open myself up to more. I'm going to call my children. I'm going to urge them to come for a visit, or I will go to them. I could board Casper for a few days, or I could tuck him in a carrier beneath my plane seat. But I can't go to them yet. First I need to see my mother. I can take a weekend to go East, then to New York to see Kira, and another to go Southwest. Unless I can get my children to come and visit me, to see the adequate little dwelling I've put together. Will they care enough to make the effort? Maybe they'd come for Christmas. I've never been alone at Christmas. I don't want to be alone.

I wipe away the tears that have started to blur my

vision. Casper cocks his head as if to ask what's wrong. I realize he's one of the few souls who has ever seen me cry. Maybe there's something wrong with that. Maybe in trying to appear strong, I've come across as cold, unapproachable. Maybe if I let people know that I need them – not that I'm needy, but that I value their role in my life – then my family will understand why it's important to connect.

* * *

Good as it was to get away it's uncommonly wonderful to be home. To walk through my door, unfasten Casper's leash, take off my jacket and toss it on a chair, and just breathe. This place is my salvation. I try not to think of my beautiful old house where so many memories were made, but it's gone, just like the family I once had. I can't get the house back, nor would I care to, but I want my children back, if even for a very short while.

My father could have given me some advice. He would have told me to insist that they come for a visit, but I'm not so sure that would work with Jordan or Kira. He never insisted I go back east for a visit after college, but I'd married Glenn and I think Dad knew he couldn't tell a couple what to do. I suppose I made it difficult for him, and it must have seemed that I didn't care about my parents. That's what I'm feeling now about my own son and daughter, that maybe they just don't care. Is that what happens in families? The ties are cut and the spell is shattered? It seems I'm the pot calling the kettle black.

I so want at least some of what I once had to continue in my life. When I was little, I felt surrounded by two doting parents. My father directed my every move while my mother was always there. She was quiet, but there, observing. Sometimes she's a bit of a conundrum. She couldn't possibly have agreed with everything he suggested. But maybe I'm more like her than I want to admit. What objections have I voiced to my own children? What unsolicited advice have I given them? And didn't I let Glenn have the final word on anything he chose to weigh in on? It's strange to look at oneself and realize the reflection from one generation to the next.

Yes, I need to not just demand more of my children. I need to demand more of myself too. I need to be a better daughter. I'll call Mother to make sure she's up for my visit, then I'll make arrangements to go there next weekend. I'll spend this week getting the files in order for the next quarter and I'll see about boarding Casper for the two or three days I'm away. He and I are new to one another; it might be easier on him this time not to put him on a plane. I'm sure he was never subjected to the fuss and noise before. I'll plan to take him with me next time.

Suddenly I have this little responsibility in a fluffy white coat. I'm thankful for him. He lost so much and so did I. We're going to get through this together, but there's no promise it will be easy.

Sitting on my new sofa with a bottle of water, my dog

at my side, his head on my lap, the fire glowing, I call my mother. I'm glad when she answers, though she definitely sounds suspicious of my motives. Maybe she has reason to. There have been times I've acted less as a daughter and more as a warden. She's surprised by my request to visit, by my suggestion that we could do a little Christmas shopping as we did when I was a teenager, but she's receptive. I tell her I'll call when my itinerary is set, and we hang up.

It might be tricky to get a flight to Boston on the holiday weekend, but now that it's just me, I can be flexible about what time I go. And hopefully there will be a rental car available.

I should be happy but the tears are flowing. and I'm glad that no one can see. I hate giving in to crying, but I am saturated with the change in my life, I feel genuinely lost. Is this my payment for moving so far away to school and then marriage? Did I do this? I did this. Why did I do this? I wouldn't trade my kids for anything, but my life has partially been in vain. I'm divorced, alone. Why did this happen? I've always tried hard to be a good student, and I was. I tried to make our house a home, and I believe I did. What then was I missing that made it all end? I'm guessing that it was because there was never a true beginning.

I need to pull myself together. I've always been self-sufficient, capable of working full time, running a household, raising two intelligent and talented children, and catering to the wishes of a husband who was never

157

fully committed to us. Did I accomplish what I'd intended? I'm not even sure if what I did was intended or if it just happened. I'm lost. Not completely, but somewhat.

I've got to ask Kira and Jordan to come for Christmas. I don't think I can get through it without them, or at least one of them. I don't know how my mother has dealt with eight years of being on her own, holidays and day after day. Her siblings are both gone, her parents gone, many of her friends are gone. She has that goat. I can't help but smooth away the tears as a smile broadens my lips. A damn goat.

Sadearah

I look in the mirror and see nice hair. It's the one thing that doesn't echo old age, except of course, for the color. Gray with a mix of white is a give-away that I'm no longer in my child-bearing days. I have good hair, though, and I'm grateful for that. It's thick and well-coiffed, thanks to Senya, my talented hairdresser. I suppose I should see her more often than every few months. I'll try for an appointment tomorrow, before Suzanna gets here. Plus I'll look nice for myself during the holidays.

I see wrinkles, lots of them all over this face, but I would not expect to see youthful smoothness. The eyes still shine and the eyelashes and brows are like what grows on my head, thick and noticeable. However I have no one to impress except myself. Henry told me often over an early morning cup of coffee or a bowl of oatmeal, that I was the most beautiful woman he'd ever seen. I'd nod and smile, but I didn't believe a word.

When my friend Meg lost her husband then married her husband's best friend, my mutterings to myself were to question her judgment. The last thing I'd do is live with another man, married or not.

Henry was part of my life from my early twenties. I can claim that I knew no better. Had I waited longer, I might have had another plan. Regrets are useless things, and if I am to be honest with myself, my life with Henry was interesting.

Being in the company of someone intelligent and determined to live a decent life is not a negative. There are so many out in this world with no one and some who have someone who is not emotionally or physically supportive. I can't complain and be justified.

My thoughts return to Stephen. It occurs to me that he's never mentioned his mother. I've been immersed in pity for the child who was compelled to create and was discouraged. Where was his other parent in this? Did his mother agree with the father? And if she did, shame on her. Tactfully, I'll have to ask him about her when he and I meet again. That probably won't be until spring, months away. I'm sorry he and I are hours apart.

Now this isn't good. I've managed to put a crack in my mirror. I was so frustrated thinking about Stephen's situation that while shaking a bottle with a combination of detergent and bleach to clean the bathroom sink, I've made a mess as it slipped out of my hand and went flying to the glass. I must try harder to be careful. I no longer have the in-house repairman as I did with Henry. He'd simply have taken the medicine chest door apart, replaced the mirror, done and done. I will need to take the door off its hinges and get Mr. Clemente to replace the mirror at his hardware store. I'm a dope for being so reckless. I'd best not have seven years of bad luck.

Having started heating some soup for supper, soon it will be time to assess the temperature in Georgie's shed. According to the thermometer, the temperature has dropped twelve degrees since noon when it was forty-four. Maybe I'll bring him inside. No sense in him being uncomfortable. He's no bother and not a bit rambunctious when in the house.

It's at times like this when I'm glad my daughter lives far away. She would, no doubt, raise the question about my sanity. Luckily the temperature this weekend is supposed to be decent, so I won't feel like I need to bring him in while she's visiting. My daughter doesn't need to know everything about my life. She'd probably analyze every detail. One way or another she'd see me as being unfit to continue living on my own. Well, I don't live on my own. I have Georgie. Humans, their voices often filled with contradiction and discouragement are so much more difficult to live with than animals.

I think I'll take one of the wool blankets from the linen closet out with me to keep Georgie comfortable for now, and if needed, I'll bring him in with another blanket or two on the kitchen floor. I won't have him subjected to the cold.

The soup, however, is not cold. It's bubbling away. As I ladle some into a bowl, and watch the steam rise, I decide to let it cool while I tend to Georgie. I take the blanket with me and head out to the shed.

The air is chilled, and I realize that I should have put on a heavier jacket, maybe even some gloves. This weather is no good for old joints.

When I open the shed door, I notice Georgie's poor old back rippling with the chill inside the shed. That settles that. Georgie is coming in. I clip on his leash and lead him to my kitchen. I give him his feed laced with pieces of broccoli and carrots, a few grapes, and one cookie, then I sit at the table to eat my soup. It's nice to share a meal with someone.

Why can't it be this easy to take care of one's children? Food, water, a warm bed, an occasional pat on the head, and some fresh air – that's all good, necessary, but it's not enough. I do wish that I knew what more to do for Suzanna. Here she is coming to stay this weekend, Thanksgiving weekend but not for Thanksgiving, having suggested we go Christmas shopping, and I'm simply baffled. This is not the daughter I've become accustomed to.

She won't let on that her life has been burdened by sorrow, by the loss of everything she's known. I lost Henry to a health issue. Suzanna lost Glenn to the man's efforts to please himself rather than the woman who encouraged his career and gave him two children. I will never understand that sort of selfishness.

My soup is too salty but hearty and warm. I take the dish to the sink, empty the remains, pat Georgie, and head to my room to change. Once in my pajamas, bathrobe, and slippers, I'm physically comfortable and emotionally stressed. I can't help but worry about Suzanna out there alone. She has that little dog, she has her cause, but when she turns out the lights at night, she must feel forsaken.

We can plan all we want to, but plans can go wrong. She must wonder what she did to deserve desertion. Not that she would necessarily want a life with a man who wanted something different, but still, it's clearly rejection.

I need to stop fretting about Suzanna's life. There's little to nothing that I can do to make a difference. What I'm going to do is make a decision for something I can manage. I'm going to have a grilled cheese sandwich with sliced tomatoes and basil leaves for my Thanksgiving dinner. I'll have an array of vegetables mingled with sliced apples for Georgie. And for dessert I'll have chocolate cake. Georgie won't.

I remember one Christmas when my father was making dinner because my mother was sick with the flu. She requested chicken noodle soup and her bed. Father asked what we would like to eat and gave us a choice. There would be no traditional dinner. Doug wanted a peanut butter sandwich and chocolate milk. Esther wanted spaghetti without sauce, just butter and parmesan cheese. I remember laughing as I requested crackers with raspberry jam and chocolate in some form. My father had some of everything the three of us kids had, and we all laughed as we promised not to tell Mother. It was the most fun we ever had at Christmas. I was seven, Esther was eleven, and Doug was fourteen. So I'm perfectly fine with Thanksgiving dinner being a gourmet version of a grilled cheese sandwich. It's going to be delicious.

When Henry died eight years ago, friends asked what I was going to do without him. I always wondered what anyone does when confronted with loss of any sort. You make the best of it. There's not much choice. I miss Henry, but I'm grateful that he died peacefully, as though he'd accepted his fate and was going quietly. It happened so fast that I barely had time to say goodbye, and I did that, holding his hand. I remember thanking him for a lovely life. I didn't know what else to say. It seemed like a time to be kind, forgiving. What else would there have been to say?

But I can't retrace the past. It is cast in stone, and it's time for me to move on. I hope that Suzanna is also able to find a new path to fulfillment. She's not the most adoring daughter, but she's a good girl and has led a noble life.

The divorce had nothing to do with her. It came from deceit though. I wonder if she would have been better off if she'd never married him. But, then, she wouldn't have Kira and Jordan. Still, I claim it was selfish on Glenn's part for so many reasons. He basically dismissed his former life, including his wife, his son, and his daughter. Terribly selfish. And maybe he couldn't help it. What good would it have done to continue living a lie? But, still, he hurt my daughter, and for that I won't forgive him. Until death do us part, a broken contract.

What I need to remember is that I am Suzanna's mother. Neither of us can alter that, and if Henry was here, he would no doubt find the proper words to mend our daughter's heart. Surely she must feel desolate, abandoned. What does one say for this loss? I suppose something similar to what is said to a grieving partner when a death occurs. I heard the words from others when Henry passed, but it was simply noise. I would have preferred dogs at my side. Dogs comfort without expecting you to reply, without thanking them for coming.

But perhaps this is just the opportunity I need. Suzanna is coming this weekend. She didn't sound like her motive is to investigate me. She sounded, in her own way, like she needs her mother.

How wonderful it would be if I could connect to her the way I do with Stephen. Even though I'm not his mother, I'm proud of him. He's managed to combine a profitable career with time to paint. He's sold several of his paintings through a gallery in Hartford, which certainly must be proof to him that his work has merit and that his father was wrong.

How incredibly thoughtless it is for a parent to damage a child's psyche, as my mother did to me. Never, ever would I murmur that horrid name to anyone.

With me having to live with it for nearly seventy years, it's as bad as it's going to get.

I must send Stephen a Christmas card. I'll find a nice one among my boxes of cards from other years, and I'll reassure him that his art is wonderful and that he should be very proud. Everyone needs positive praise, and I am sincere. Stephen's work is splendid, a wonderful glimpse into his soul. I believe that to be true of all artists, painters, writers, musicians. I wonder if they realize what they add to our mundane duties in life. There's so much we need to do that has no element of fun or enrichment. We are expected to work, day after day, doing what we might not choose to do with our time. I enjoyed being an editor for textbooks, but given the choice, I'd have been knitting colorful mittens instead.

Yes, a nice card and note will go out to Stephen a week or so before Christmas. And I'll send cards to Suzanna, Jordan, and Kira with checks to buy something they'd enjoy. I'm out of ideas for gifts, though maybe Suzanna will have some. It was always easier to buy something for her as a teenager when she was with me to pick it out. And of course it was so much easier when I could buy teddy bears and cute outfits for the grandkids and a silver necklace or earrings for Suzanna.

There were times when I found lovely silk ties for Glenn, and now there will never again be a thought for something to buy for him. Not that I'm angry for his decision. He may have tried to conform, to make his union with Suzanna work. I'm just a bit miffed that he married her when he must have known his preference. It wasn't fair. I'm disappointed in the father of my grandchildren.

Suzanna

I cannot believe that Thanksgiving is in two days. I have the desserts to make that I promised to Joe for his gathering. I thought at first that it would be fun, a nice mix of people, but now I find myself regretting accepting the invitation.

I should have planned to go to my mother's for the entire holiday weekend rather than arrive the day after. Is this what my life will be comprised of, celebrating an important holiday with people I barely know?

Sometimes I feel a little sick thinking how much of my former life is just gone. Traditions are lost. Maybe that's why I'm looking forward to some Christmas shopping with my mother this weekend. We always did that when I was growing up. In fact, I think it's the only thing my mother ever really seemed joyous about.

Perhaps that's what we come to when we become wives and mothers – what everyone else wants. And now that my husband and children have left, all that I have here that I care about is my little Casper. He brings me joy. He's happy to see me each time I walk into the house – even if I've just gone out to get the mail, and he's by my side every time I sit down. I've missed not having a pet. Why did I accept everything Glenn said? I could have made a point that I was often alone and a pet would have been a companionable comfort. I let too much go Glenn's way.

I probably should have addressed Thanksgiving itself with my mother. I'll call her in the morning while my pie is in the oven. I don't know what I'll say to her other than happy Thanksgiving. She didn't ask me to come for the holiday, so I suppose she's content with whatever plans she has. I never know with her. But I'm hopeful that we can enjoy the weekend. And I still can't believe she has a goat.

My Green Space co-workers have told me that I've managed to organize them in a way they never knew before. I'm efficient at making schedules, contacts, files that are in order and easy to comprehend. I love that I'm making a difference.

I've also been told that no one there has a specific agenda or schedule. If you want to work three days a week, that's acceptable. If you want to take a week off, that is also agreeable. Next time I go east, I'll take Casper with me. But I'm happy that this time I can leave him with Joe for the weekend. Casper will enjoy being at Joe's. They get along well, and I'm sure Casper will enjoy some of the turkey. I'll put my suitcase in the car, go to the festivities, enjoy the company there, and then head to the airport. It'll be fun to surprise my mother with an earlier flight. It's all working out.

Yes, just this once, I'll leave Casper with Joe.

* * *

The call to my mother was brief. She sounded alert and was expecting to have her dinner in the early afternoon. She didn't say what she was preparing, but she was always a decent cook, so I expect a bit of chicken and stuffing, potatoes, and her much loved butternut squash. She seemed enthused about the day, but no one was joining her. She didn't seem to mind.

I wonder how she's managed to feel content on her own. Dad was always mulling about the kitchen on Thanksgiving. He liked to cook a bit and always assembled a wonderful tray of fruit and nuts. He was good at making biscuits, too. Those were some wonderful meals that the two of them put together.

* * *

Joe's gathering was interesting. I liked everyone there, even though the food was a bit more California than I had ever adapted to. The tray of pineapple and grapes was beautiful, very artistic. The cold meat platter surrounded with potato slices dressed in celery seed and olive oil was interesting. Everything was surprisingly delicious, yet it seemed more like summer fare than I had expected. The one change I didn't make when married and living the California dream was the typical New England food I prepared for the holidays. Glenn never complained. In fact, he seemed to love the old-fashioned stuffing and thick gravy over his mashed potatoes. The kids liked it as well.

As I drive to the airport, I decide that for Christmas I'll forego any invitations and remain home to make Casper, the kids and me a nice roasted chicken with all the fixings. My mother will most likely prepare something similar for herself, and perhaps that goat.

When I get home, I should put up a tree, a tiny tree with little lights and some cheerful ornaments.

Who am I kidding? This is going to be a terrible Christmas. I know Kira and Jordan are going to say they're busy. I'm going to be alone.

I hate these damn tears. I hate that I miss what I had. I'll put up a tree anyway, and I'll make dinner for Casper and me. And I'll sit home and watch old movies and sob. The movies will be my excuse.

I wonder if my mother still puts up a tree. She had one up every year the day after Thanksgiving. I thought it was too early, but Dad let her do it. He'd bring the tree inside, set it in a stand with water, place the lights, then it was hers. He'd take a cup of coffee into the kitchen and sit in his rocking chair reading the newspaper while she decorated. I likely hung out in my bedroom, doing whatever was age appropriate. Later, Dad would call to me to come see the tree. He and I would look at it and my mother would have this smile on her face as she'd look up at the star. My father always said it was very nice. I don't remember if I said *anything*.

Perhaps I'll see if she wants to put up a tree while I'm there this weekend. Why not?

Sadearah

Well, I think this Thanksgiving was fine. I had my wonderful grilled cheese, tomato and basil sandwich. Georgie had his vegetables in with his feed, and he spent the night on his kitchen rug.

The years of putting up a real tree are gone. I was never enthused about killing a lovely balsam, but Henry insisted we needed a freshly cut tree. I don't know why he cared so much, but to get my tree up early, I accepted his decision without a protest. Now my little two-foot high artificial tree does the trick. I'll put that up later today, before Suzanna arrives tomorrow afternoon. She'll likely think it ridiculous, but I simply am beyond the point of needing any approval.

In the meanwhile, I need to clean out Georgie's shed and pack it with fresh hay. But even if it isn't cold tonight, I think I'll bring him back in. I'm sure he'd love to see my little tree, all the sweet lights and pretty ornaments. We're going to have a wonderful Christmas.

I believe I'll buy a nice little bell for Georgie's blue collar, and I'll make sure he has all kinds of fruits. He adores bananas, and apples are always welcome. Every living thing should know joy. I'll buy extra bird seed for the birds and squirrels, and I'll pick up a few bags of unsalted peanuts for them as well.

I miss Henry in many ways, and I wish Suzanna and I were close. But I feel that I have it all right here in this little beach house where my life is not governed by anyone or anything. I am so fortunate. So many friends Henry and I shared in Jamaica Plain have ended up moving to Florida and wishing they hadn't, being tended to in nursing homes, or are in their graves. And here I am, living free as a bird and feeling fine. At the age of eighty-two I believe I have longevity in me and that I'll be right here ten years from now. That's my Christmas wish, to be here with Georgie, or with some little animal orphan of some sort for many years to come.

After my tree is up later today, I'll sit down with a good cup of coffee and write a few cards. After that, I'll see about bringing Georgie inside. I'm sure he'd prefer the kitchen to the shed, and I will appreciate his company.

I can't help but smile when I think of what my mother would say to my keeping company with a goat. She was quite the fuss – floors gleaming, furniture polished, dishes practically boiled to prevent any germs. She would be horrified with Georgie in the kitchen. I suppose no one in my family, or even among friends, would approve of a goat in the house. I don't care.

While I'm writing cards, I have to remember to make

one out for Stephen. I'll write him a little note, wishing him a wonderful winter. I'll include that I hope to see him in the spring.

I find it interesting that in my long and lovely life I have had a family and I have known many friends. But it took me nearly eighty-two years to find someone with whom I feel at home. Stephen is a gentle soul with a strong fortitude. I admire his ability to adjust to disappointments in both his marriage and his father.

His work is brilliantly appealing, he's successful, yet in addition to painting, he holds down an important position which affords him a nice home and all he's determined he needs. He loves his son, sees him often, and is paying for a good school. If I'd had a son, I would have been proud of a boy like Stephen. I must remember in spring to ask about his mother.

* * *

My tree is up and glorious. I've had chocolate cake and my nice hot coffee, I've written my cards and Georgie is resting on the rug, his large eyes feasting on the little tree right in the center of my kitchen table. It's beautiful.

I thought I'd feel joyful, and I do to some extent, but it's all mingled with melancholy. I miss so many good people, and Henry is first on that list. Even if he didn't love me best, I had a memorable friendship with him and a life I would repeat. I'm sorry he's not here with me. I think I could have persuaded him to allow Georgie into the warmth of the kitchen. He wasn't a cruel man.

He'd have understood.

And I think about the little girl I bought dolls and teddy bears for, and pink ribbons for her lovely hair. I remember how she danced around the kitchen for her father, her legs attempting to pirouette, her little body twirling. She was once filled with glee, and I don't know why that ended. I always smiled at her endeavors and expressed my delight in her accomplishments. I'm so angry with Glenn for his deceptive life. He's certainly injured my child. The oddity is, that while I am reluctant to spend time with Suzanna, if she needed a new heart to live, I would gladly relinquish my own.

Ah, well, I am doing just fine. I love this little house, I love my little tree, I love my pal, Georgie, and I love my friendship with Stephen. I can't redo the past. I can't make some memories fade while others come forward. What I have in this moment is supremely wonderful and I will proceed in being grateful. And I will hope that my time with my daughter is a rebirth of what can be.

Suzanna and Sadearah

What an interesting place my mother has chosen to make her home. I hesitate before knocking at her door then decide no, I'm her daughter, I don't need to knock. I walk in and there before my eyes is my mother in her bathrobe having a cup of coffee while reading a small newspaper, and Lord Almighty, the goat is on the kitchen rug.

"Suzanna, what in the world are you doing here at seven in the morning?"

"The time is an issue?"

"Yes, of course it is. I thought you planned to be here later this afternoon."

"I was able to get an earlier flight." I set my travel bag and purse on a chair near the goat then move both, afraid he might eat them. "It made more sense, less travelers to deal with." I stand looking from her to the goat.

"Had you let me know you were coming, I'd have prepared something more substantial for you than this cranberry muffin. Will you have one with coffee?"

176

I sit down in a chair near to her. With the Christmas tree in the center of the table, I'd have been staring at it rather than her if I'd sat directly across from her. My mother seemed to do everything in life upside down and inside out. The tree was pretty, but in the middle of everything?

"I'll have coffee, but no muffin. Thank you."

I watch as she stands, walks to the coffee pot, selects a cup and saucer for me, then pours the black brew into it.

"You still take it black, no sugar?" she asked.

"Yes. Are we going to discuss the elephant, or rather the goat, in the room, Mother?"

"It's cold in the shed," she says nonchalantly as she places my cup and saucer down then sits across from me.

"He's a barn animal. They're used to the cold."

"And is there a reason why they should get *used* to the cold?"

"Don't you think it's a little strange to have a goat in your home?"

She laughs. "I guess I don't think it's at all strange, Suzanna. Actually, what I think is strange is you showing up, unannounced, at my door early in the morning. Did you have a reason why you didn't inform me that you were coming earlier than planned for a visit?"

I look at her and take a few sips of hot coffee. "It was a spur of the moment decision. Carpe diem."

"Where's your little dog?"

"He's with a friend. Maybe I'll bring him next time."

"The dog or the friend?" my mother asked with a mischievous grin.

There was a period of silence between us. My mother seems to be waiting for more words to flow from me, but that isn't an answer I'm prepared to give.

She must sense my discomfort and changes the subject. "Did you have a nice Thanksgiving?"

"Yes. I was with mostly Green Space people at my friend's home. It was entertaining, enjoyable, different. And you?"

"Georgie and I had a fine Thanksgiving. Have your return plans changed?"

"No. Would you mind if I take a shower and change my clothes?"

"Go right ahead. The guest room is ready. I'll get dressed while you're showering. You're looking well, Suzanna."

I'm not sure how to respond to that statement, yet I find myself feeling acceptance. I take my shower, change to slacks and a shirt, then walk into the kitchen where my mother is giving the goat slices of apple.

She'd changed into slacks and a dark blue blouse, her silver hair settled around her shoulders. I'm not sure I ever noticed before that her hair style seems fairly youthful for a woman in her eighties. She actually looks stunning, her eyes bright with living, and her body seeming agile.

"Did you have plans for today?" she asks as she turns toward me.

I sit down again at the table. "I came for a visit, but I'm open to doing something out or staying here. Did you have plans for today?"

My mother gives the goat his last slice of apple then turns back to me. "I almost never make plans. When I run out of a particular item, like flour, sugar, coffee, I go to the store. Sometimes I go to the goat farm and help out. The folks there are getting on in age, somewhere in their sixties. They appreciate a little help now and then."

I almost laugh. This woman is considering the age of the goat farmers who are closer to my age than hers. I wondered if she's thinking clearly. Does she remember that she's in her eighties now?

"Well, I'm not much for goat farming, but maybe we can find something else to do. I haven't seen the Atlantic in a while. What would you think of lunch and a ride someplace – your choice."

Mother smiles and I wonder what is going on in that mind of hers.

"The Atlantic is about fifty feet from my back door. But why not take a jaunt? We could drive to the National Seashore and then have lunch at McClary's. You used to like that place when you were young. Your father liked it, too."

I look at her and can't resist asking, "What about you? Do you like it at McClary's?"

She shrugs her shoulders and says, "They have good

179

chowder."

I understand, noting her expression that she went to that restaurant because my father favored it. His seafood choice was a good haddock with mashed potatoes and carrots. I preferred the whole belly clams and French fries. I couldn't recall what my mother ever ordered there. My father insisted on my input to most everything, but my mother tended to be still, as though observing how I would react to a request or expected behavior. I don't think I was difficult, but I also wasn't particularly engaged.

"Good," I say. "I like chowder, too. Let's go there and to the seashore. I haven't been in years."

I can envision my father there, and it is going to be a distinct change. So much of who we were as a family depended on him serving as navigator. Our journey to the seashore would have been planned to include photography, his hobby, and then maybe a wrangling ride through one of the narrow old roads. I was most often in the car's back seat reading. Disconnecting, I suppose.

We leave the goat in the kitchen with a bucket of water and feed, finish the last sips of our coffee, then head out to my rented car.

The drive was a rambling half hour and now I wonder what she's thinking as her eyes scan the windows of the restaurant and then the length of beach at the shore. Certainly she is reflecting as I am that nothing is quite the same without Dad. He never stopped. He was always explaining what was off in the distance, the history of the lighthouses, and how some of the greenery survived harsh storms and winter's cold. I remember that well, yet at the time, before college, I doubt I was paying much attention. In fact, I try to recall what I was thinking other than making an escape to something of my own, such as the West Coast. I was most likely exercising my teen enthusiasm for being an individual, completely free of doting parents, or at least a doting father. I always knew that I mattered to him. I'm not sure I thought I had that attention from my mother. I'm still not sure.

When our crocks of chowder arrive, I watch as she takes a little spoonful, then adds some pepper, then the oyster crackers. I do the same. The rest of our meal is filled with an occasional comment about a gull or the weather. Nothing heavy and nothing intimate. No more than two strangers would have to discuss.

The check arrives and she insists on paying. This is a different side of her. I ask if I can at least leave the tip, and she nods. Then we head back to the car and she directs me where to go.

"Do you go out for rides like this in California?" she asks as I drive.

"No, not really. Having lived there for thirty years, I know the area pretty well. I've always just kept busy with work and home."

"And you're enjoying your little dog."

"Yes."

181

The next half hour is filled with beautiful views but there isn't much conversation. We pull into my mother's soft sand driveway. I think about my gravel parking area in my once-upon-a-time house, and the gravel I'd had spread down at my new place. It occurs to me that my mother and I are living in similar abodes, small and casual. My parents had a magnificent home in JP and I had a show-stopper before the divorce. Both of us had made changes we hadn't anticipated.

Walking into my mother's kitchen, we look at the goat as he maneuvers himself to a standing position. He'd eaten his feed and looked at us as if he hoped for a treat.

"Hello, Dear Georgie," my mother says. "I'll get you a banana in just a minute. Let me hang up my coat."

In a narrow closet my mother slips her coat onto a hanger and leaves the door open for me to do the same. She then fetches the banana, peels it, and gives it to her friend. I watch with interest as the tenderness is visible. This is my mother's companion, and who am I to judge? I have Casper and I enjoy taking good care of him.

"I'm going out to the shed to collect some hay," she informs me. "He'll be staying in tonight, and he's had enough feed. I was going to put him back out in the shed, but he does like it in here."

"Do you want me to get the hay?"

My mother shakes her head no. "I know how much, and it won't take long. Make yourself comfortable."

She no sooner leaves the house with a sweater

wrapped around her shoulders when the phone rings. I hesitate then pick it up. "Hello?"

"Hi. Is Sadearah there please?"

"I'm afraid you have the wrong number. There's no one by that name here."

A hesitation ensued. Then he repeated the number twice, which was my mother's.

"May I ask who's calling?"

"Yes, of course. My name is Stephen and my friend gave me this number."

"Your friend?"

"Yes, she's an older lady who was from Winderlee, Connecticut."

I hesitate before replying. "My mother had grandparents there."

Another hesitation. "Is your mother silver-haired? I'm sorry, I don't mean to be persistent, but I had hoped to connect with Sadearah."

As I listen, my mother walks into the kitchen with an armful of hay which she places before Georgie. She looks at me with the phone in my hands and waits for me to explain.

"Do you know anyone named Sadearah?" I ask.

My mother blushes then reaches for the phone. "I'll take it," she says with no explanation. I sit down at the kitchen table and listen to my mother speaking to a man I do not know. It's curious to see her smile as she listens and then to hear her say she'd love that. Love what?

When she places the phone back on its receiver, she

straightens the goat's hay and adds a slice or two of apple. After fussing with this and that, avoiding me nicely, she finally asks if I'd like a heated up cup of coffee. I say yes. She heats two and then sits down a foot away from me.

"Mother, who is this person he asked for? And who is he?"

She sips her coffee and then looks at me, almost defiantly. The silvery color of her eyes, the pale eyelashes and eyebrows, become illuminated by late afternoon sun slipping into the kitchen. She truly is beautiful.

"That was Stephen. I met him at a café in Connecticut about a year ago. We've become friends."

"Really. How old is this man?"

My mother looks away toward the goat and then shrugs. "About your age, I'd guess."

I'm not sure what to say. "And what is this relationship about?" I ask carefully.

My mother looks directly at me. "Goodness, Suzanna. Obviously you're suspicious that it's something other than what it is. We are friends, that's all. Although I should not use the words *that's all*. We're *good* friends. I like him very much. We enjoy having a bite to eat together when I go down to Connecticut."

I'm quiet, waiting for more information. She doesn't offer anything else. "That's nice. So, why did he call?"

"He asked how my Thanksgiving was and I said fine."

184

"What else did he say?"

Again my mother looks directly at me as if I have some nerve asking all these questions.

"He asked what I was doing over Christmas. He asked me to think about him coming up for the day from Connecticut."

"On Christmas?" I'm astounded and I'm sure I look frustrated.

"Yes, of course. Why not? He's a lovely person and neither of us has other plans. He'll drive up for dinner and then he plans to return to Connecticut that evening. I don't know why you seem bothered by it. This doesn't impact you at all. You have your children and your new friends. Without Stephen I'd be here, alone except for Georgie. Georgie will enjoy the company, too, I'm sure."

"Does this Stephen know about Georgie?"

"Of course he does, Suzanna. And, yes, he knows I bring him inside when it's cold."

I digest that piece of information and then ask, "Why did he ask for someone named Sadearah?"

My mother looks around the kitchen, rests her eyes on Georgie for a long moment, then focuses on me with determination in her eyes. "That's how he knows me. I always hated the name Charlene. I invented the name Sadearah for myself when I was fifteen."

I allow myself a minute or two to let that sink in. "So, he doesn't know your real name?"

She looked from her coffee to me. "Sadearah is more

real to me than Charlene ever was."

"Did Dad call you Sadearah? I seem to remember him calling you *Dear*."

"No one called me Sadearah because I kept it to myself."

I stare at my coffee wondering what else I don't know about my mother. She had selected, or rather invented a name for herself. That was innovative on her part.

"You have my full permission to change your own name," she offers. "Your father named you."

I notice my mother's hair – how it rests against her shoulders and the way it glistens. "Dad named me?"

"Yes, he thought it was a perfect name." My mother squirms a bit in her chair then takes a long swallow of coffee.

"You had no name in mind for me?"

"I had thought of a few."

"Did you mention them to Dad?"

She hesitates then stares through a window to the setting sun before replying. "I liked the name Peter for a boy, Nicole or Sasha for a girl."

"What did Dad think of those names?"

"I never mentioned them. He had spoken of the name John for a boy, Suzanna for a girl. To your father I was the oven and he was the baker. I didn't resist. Later I wished I had."

I think about what she is relaying to me and wonder about this woman who gave in to her husband's wishes. Dad ran our family. No wonder it seemed we were falling apart without him. Or had we never really been together? I wasn't sure, and now I am giving thought to wonder if I had a part in my own marriage failure. Certainly I couldn't help Glenn's choice to go, but he'd stayed at my side for thirty years. What changed? Did he meet someone who he simply could not resist? When I think of him living in Japan, a place I've never been, I have this dark feeling that he's in outer space with an unknown.

My mother interrupts my thoughts. "Did you like growing up with that name?"

Georgie, now meticulously cleaning his front legs and chest, captivates my attention and makes me smile before I turn back to her. "I never thought about it really. It didn't occur to me to change it. But it sounds like *you* had regrets about my name. Is that so?"

My mother stands, takes our empty cups to the sink, and washes them, leaving them on the drain board upside down. She turns and glances at me as if I might be a piece of dust she should sweep away. "I had questions," she answers simply.

"Such as?"

"I'm not sure I want to get this conversation going. Maybe another time."

I watch as she gives the goat a few green beans then tops it off with another thick slice of apple.

"What do you think you'd like for supper?" she asks. "We had an early lunch, so you must be getting hungry."

"We could go out," I suggest.

187

"We did that today already. What would you think of chicken pot pie? I have a good sized one in the freezer. I could thaw it in the microwave then bake it in the oven."

I stand and walk to the back door where I flip on the outside light. "Pot pie sounds great for a chilly evening like this. Is the goat staying in again?"

"If you were in charge, would you put him out in the cold?"

I think about Casper with his thick little coat of fur. No, I would put nothing out to suffer the discomfort of cold. "No, I wouldn't," I confess.

My mother's back is to me, but I see her shoulders relax, and I have the feeling she's smiling.

* * *

That evening after a delicious meal and a cup of hot cider, I feel relaxed for the first time in months. I look over at my mother who is tucked neatly into a roomy chair with a blanket over her knees. The goat is settled down for the night and I am tired.

"What was it about my name you weren't enthused about?" I ask.

My mother closes her eyes for a few seconds then opens them to stare toward her Christmas tree just a few feet from where we sit.

"I think it's getting late and we should probably get some rest."

I decide to let go of the question, and two days later after a little Christmas shopping on Small Business Saturday and a lot more getting to learn about this woman who's known me my whole life, I am on my way back to California, assured that my mother is fine for the time being. She may even be better off than me.

Sadearah

Suzanna's visit was surprisingly enjoyable. She said nothing of what she was doing for Christmas, and I kept my mouth shut. Maybe she wants a quiet day, the first Christmas without Glenn. And maybe she has the kids coming, or maybe she'll be seeing friends again. Whatever she is doing, it isn't with me, but I'm used to that now.

* * *

It's just three days before Christmas, and I'm excited that Stephen is coming here for dinner. I've asked what he'd prefer to eat, and he said a sandwich of any sort will do, it's more about the company we keep. There's something special about that young man. And he knows Georgie will be here and told me that he's actually looking forward to meeting him. Georgie will be thrilled.

I've baked and frozen my chocolaty brownies as well as an apple tart, and I have both chocolate and vanilla ice cream for either or both of them. The meal will be delicious and a little more than sandwiches – Delmonico potatoes, one of those nice little roasted chickens from the store, a garden salad, and some of my old fashioned baking powder biscuits. We'll have hot cider, and maybe even a shot of good whiskey. Henry liked to have some once in a while. Whatever we have, it will be perfect. The feast is planned and won't be a fuss.

I've also knit Stephen a scarf and matching hat using this magnificent multi-colored yarn in subtle hues of reds and golds. It reminds me of the coloring in his artwork, of the autumn foliage. Georgie's bell for his collar is wrapped, and I've bought Georgie more apples. He'll be given a biscuit or two while Stephen and I eat our meal as well. He may even have some salad, hold the dressing. Christmas Eve day I will drop off a bushel of apples to the goats at the farm. They too deserve a little treat.

I have the distinct feeling that this is going to be one of my best ever Christmases. I have no reason to hide anything from Stephen. He and I do not have a history. We're friends, no expectations. I wish I could feel this relaxed about spending time with my daughter, but she is, in fact, a person who sees other's defects and not her own. At her age and mine, it's likely too late to correct, though her last visit was a start. Our relationship is enveloped and tarnished with misinterpretation as well as a lifetime of what was. Sometimes it is difficult to get beyond that, to open up to those we are closest to. I will help her if she needs my help. I believe she would do the same for me. But beyond that, my guess is that there is nothing.

* * *

Arriving at noon from Connecticut, Stephen steps into my kitchen carrying a nicely wrapped package about two feet long, a foot high, and three or four inches deep. I have hopes that it is possibly one of his paintings. I open it and cry. It is a wonderful rendition of my grandparents' farm in Winderlee.

I give him his package and he immediately wraps the gold and red scarf around his neck then pulls the hat into place over his thick dark hair.

We feed Georgie then sit down to a warm and very good meal. Stephen is delighted with the Delmonico potatoes and asks if he can take some back to Connecticut with him. I package up the remainder and place them with his coat.

We talk and later have our desserts, samplings of both with ice cream. I brew us fresh coffee and I offer the whiskey which he refuses.

"Your family was not to be a destination today?" I ask.

"I saw my son last night, but his mother has him today. And my father and the rest, they're actually in Florida. I haven't spent Christmas with them in years. They do untraditional things. One year they all went on a cruise." He smiles but it is not a smile revealing happiness.

I let the silence settle in and then ask, "You've mentioned your father to me, but not your mother."

Stephen's expression sobers. "She was sick most of her life. After giving birth to my brother, her third and last child, she had a stroke. She was just thirty-two. From that time on, we were looked after by an aunt and then my father when he came home from work. My mother died when I was sixteen."

"I'm so sorry, Stephen."

He looks at me and reaches over to pat my shoulder lightly. In separate, comfortable old chairs, we fasten our eyes to the Christmas tree and say no more.

When he leaves to return to Connecticut, I give him a container of brownies, most of the apple tart, and those Delmonico potatoes he so enjoyed. He thanks me for the warm scarf and hat set, and I thank him with a hug for my wonderful painting.

When I watch his car pull out of my driveway, I walk to the remaining apple tart and give it to Georgie. High in spirit, I am in awe of this joy-filled day, and then I wonder how Suzanna's Christmas was spent.

Suzanna

I have never felt so alone. With my hand on Casper's little body, his dark brown eyes gazing at the small tree I have by my front door, I feel as though Christmas never happened.

Joe invited me to go with him to his sister's home thirty miles away and I declined. He didn't argue the point, and I was relieved. No one else here even knew that I would be alone.

Kira was going skiing in Vermont with her boyfriend and others. Jordan was again traveling to Seattle to be with Michael's family. God only knows where Glenn ended up. I feel inordinately empty.

I've thought to call my mother, but she has that Stephen there for dinner, and she has her goat. Maybe I'll call her later, or tomorrow. What can I say to her that wasn't said on my last visit? She's certainly full of surprises. I don't feel like talking to anyone just now. This day is turning out to be among the worst.

So far I've had nothing to eat and it's after four. Maybe later I'll have a can of chicken noodle soup. The days of preparing a Christmas feast are gone. I'll bet my mother made her friend a wonderful meal. She would be horrified if she knew I had nothing. I don't care. I can't wait for this day to be over.

I've been trying not to think of years past when my father was alive and insisted that we sing carols and drink his homemade eggnog. I hated that stuff, way too rich and laden with rum, or sometimes bourbon. My mother always made herself a cup of tea or had a little white wine.

The entire season was dotted with friends stopping in and family gathered around the dinner table. It was festive, I must admit, but there was no one my age at these gatherings, and I usually did my polite gig then went to my room. Even upstairs with my door closed, I could hear the music and the laughter. I thought it might be that way with Glenn and the kids, but they never took to the merrymaking. Jordan was into classical music, nothing playful. Kira, as I remember, was much like me as a teen. She often drifted away to her room early on Christmas Eve and again Christmas night. It seems we weren't much fun.

I cannot wait for this day and evening to sink into the old year. I am alone, exactly as I hoped I would not be. Glenn could have called to wish me a Merry Christmas. He hasn't called – not today, not at all, and I have no idea where he is. Not that I'd want him back. He's a cardboard figure I never knew. Good looking, tall, impressive education and career, but an imposter. This man was supposed to be, and promised to be, a devoted husband and father. While I understand our situation changing, wasn't all of our time together worth something? Friendship? Companionship? Anything worth keeping in touch for? It wasn't as if we had a nasty divorce. Both of us were civil. Why am I so easy to leave?

Was I doing all that I should? I kept a nice house, I cooked good meals, I searched for the proper colleges for our children, we took them places where their imaginations could grow and their interests were discovered. Jordan loved the museums, Kira loved theatre performances. We made certain that they were exposed to the culture each of them preferred. So, what happened? I find it disheartening that they made plans to be elsewhere for Christmas when they knew their father would not be here. They accepted that I would be alone. I don't think I understand that. Or maybe they figured I'd, like them, find other people to be with. Obviously they don't know me very well. I've never had my mother's ease at making friends.

I'll call my mother tomorrow and see how her day went. It's pretty unreal that a woman in her eighties probably had more fun than I did. Actually, *everyone* must have had more fun than me.

Sadearah

Yesterday with Stephen was one of the most memorable and cherished Christmases I can recall. Henry made the holidays joyful with his insistence for music and spiked drinks, and he often made me laugh when he'd consumed one too many rum-laced eggnogs. But yesterday was filled with good conversations, nice food and thoughtful gifts. I cherish the painting from Stephen of the old farm in Winderlee. Today I will hang it in a prominent spot.

I felt bad when Suzanna called this morning and told me that she'd spent Christmas quietly, her children off on their own. It's not my place to say anything to Kira and Jordan about abandoning their mother at Christmas, but then again, I've faced the same since Henry passed. What is the matter with this family? Somewhere along the way we've lost ourselves to a singular path. I wish it wasn't so, but I think we've given up trying to find one another.

Georgie has been good company today. It's far too cold in the shed. He's an older fellow, and why should I leave him out there alone? His absence would leave *me* alone as well.

I feel for Suzanna. She's not used to this alone stuff. I've been used to it all my life. I didn't expect it when I was married and had a child. I thought everything would be different. It wasn't different at all. Maybe when Henry and I were first married, but once Suzanna came, it was like I'd been put off to the side and for Henry it was all about raising an intelligent, happy little girl.

Thankfully over the years I had a pet or two and I had my love of knitting and reading along with my work. I've been busy enough to not feel terrible about the tightening of a life that must have seemed full and engrossing to others. I learned to live with objects, to extract joy from what I did and what I learned. The mirth I expected was nowhere to be found. Yet everyone around me seemed fulfilled, so who was I to complain?

I must write a note to Stephen. I'll do my best to explain how much I love my gift. When he called and asked about coming here for Christmas, I thought it was an unusually long hike to do on that special holiday, but I wasn't going to refuse the company of a wonderful young man. Now I realize that he wanted to give this treasured painting to me. I have yet to receive my card and gift from Suzanna. She said it's in the mail. I've heard nothing from Jordan and Kira. What is this world coming to when grandchildren don't know if you're still breathing?

It just may be that it's difficult to relate to me since

we lived so far apart. If they'd grown up closer to Henry and me, they might have given us more thought. Henry always asked Suzanna how they were and what they were doing. I think he felt somewhat disheartened by their lack of communication.

I don't think we saw them more than ten times as they were growing up. Now they're adults. They have good jobs and money of their own. They could come here to the Cape and enjoy the area as well as pay me a visit. I won't delude myself though. I know they won't come. If they can find it in their being to leave their mother alone on Christmas, there's certainly no hope of them visiting me. And, again, what would we say to one another? It would be forced, uncomfortable. Not like it is with Stephen, someone who's genuinely interesting and warm. To them I would only be an obligation.

The sun has slipped into the ocean, and I need to clean the area around my Georgie then fill his feed bucket. Since I've chosen to have a simple little salad, I'll give him some of that. And I'll have one of my lovely biscuits with butter, warmed of course. Georgie can have one of those as well.

I walked around this small house earlier with Stephen's painting, looking for its perfect home. I ended up with it in the kitchen, where I spend most of my time. It's perfectly in view from my living room too. It looks splendid there, over a small marble counter where I have a little lamp. From my favorite chair, I'm just about eight feet away from my beloved farm.

199

It must have been sometime around seven, after dinner, that I sat down in my chair with a blanket over my knees and fell asleep. At a bit before nine the phone rang. It was Stephen calling to thank me for a wonderful Christmas. He told me that he'd consumed the Delmonico potatoes and a biscuit with a steak and was preparing to have one or two of the little brownies with coffee when we finished our call. His presence in my life was fairly new and a gift, what I expected when getting married and preparing to have a family. Some things simply don't work out the way your mind plans.

Before I switch on the TV for a bit of noise and evidence of life, I decide to turn on the outside lights. I am drawn to the brilliant moonlight on the water, the way it casts a glow to everything outside.

The new teak bench is bathed in radiance, making it appear to be silver rather than the wood that it is. I could stand at the door's window and watch that moon's determined painting skills, but the right knee is a bit sore and I'll gratefully succumb to my chair and the blanket once again.

What a lovely Christmas I've had this year. Certainly it's been one of the best. I am saddened to believe that for my daughter it was one of the worst.

Suzanna

As I expected my mother had a remarkably good Christmas. She told me that Stephen had given her a painting of the old place in Connecticut. I'm not sure why she likes that farm so much, but to each his own. Meanwhile, I sit here thinking how I just mailed her a pretty assortment of soaps and a card which she should get in a day or two. I'm not strong about getting things mailed in a timely fashion. It would have been easier if she'd picked out something when we shopped that day, but it wasn't like it used to be. We were together, but separate.

I'm glad Christmas is over. I'll leave the tree up for a while. It's the only light I have on in the house. Sometimes it's just more soothing to sit in semi-darkness, where even the furniture disappears and no one knows if you're home. I'm in no mood to entertain. I'm thankful for Casper's silent companionship.

* * *

Here in the calm of night I've been propelled into consciousness with the shrill of my phone. Jordan?

Kira? No, a number I don't recognize. The voice at the other end is a woman telling me that she is a doctor. Glenn is a patient in her hospital. He has overdosed and is coming out of a critical condition, the reason for her call.

Glenn, overdosed? It's unimaginable. The man never took as much as an aspirin. I had questions and she gave me answers. The doctor had Glenn's permission to tell me what happened.

I listened intently, mystified as my former husband's condition was related to me. Discreetly the doctor told me enough that I understood – Glenn's relationship, the one he abandoned me for, was over.

I was asked if I would go, if I'd visit him as he made an effort to recover. He isn't in Japan. He's in a hospital not two hours away from me.

Off the phone, basic information written down, I sit and wonder what my place is supposed to be in his life going forward. While I was feeling abandoned on Christmas day, I had pictured my former husband with his new partner having Cosmopolitans and Martinis. I pictured him sitting by a pool in a plush hotel having forgotten that he'd fathered two children who didn't care much about either of us. I felt numb.

I lightly scratch Casper's ears and wonder if I want to get involved in Glenn's recovery. Our relationship is shattered, there's no mending that would accomplish what the doctor indicated. He was apparently a fragmented man who had left an injured wife to recover on her own or not. Where was his compassion for me, and what can I say to him concerning his circumstances? Everything over the past year has felt complicated, spoiled. My marriage is gone, my house is gone, my children are gone, and evidently Glenn was never there.

I need time. I can't make a decision to become part of his life again. He's asked for me, and in some respects I understand that. We were with one another longer than we were with anyone else.

I suppose I should inform our children. They're both away enjoying the holiday, but when they're back to their everyday lives, I'll call them. And I'll tell my mother at some point. I can't think straight right now.

Sadearah

In mulling over the conversation between Stephen and me on Christmas I came to understand that no one has it easy. Family or not, we are individuals with varied ideals.

Stephen's had his own issues with his father. And he told me that his sister lives with her millionaire husband, a life many would look at and envy, yet she confided in her brother that she feels without purpose. Being her husband's companion is not enough for her, but for him, for appearances, it is a necessity. How awful to feel deprived of using your initiative to accomplish something that matters.

His brother, who had lived well while his mother remained ill for several years after his birth, existed with the guilt of having caused his family to divide. Once a successful stockbroker, he now lives on liquor and depends on the daily opioids he pays for dearly.

Spending Thanksgiving with them was more than enough for Stephen. Surely they must all wonder what life would have been like had their mother lived.

Certainly the father had not managed cohesiveness. I wonder if most men do.

I find myself praying, which is not the usual for me, for Stephen's happiness. He's lost so much and yet he is thoughtful and kind. As I look at him as a son, I wonder if he thinks of me as a mother figure. Had that woman lived to see her children grow to adulthood, I'm certain she would have applauded their accomplishments, and maybe she'd have advised her daughter to do something other than be a rich man's wife. There is no self-esteem in that position.

Stephen and I are in agreement that when spring arrives, we'll meet again in Winderlee for a meal and conversation. That's something to look forward to. He also mentioned that he'd like a summer visit to the Cape, which would be lovely. He likes the area near Sandwich where he once stayed at a bed and breakfast. I was tempted to ask if that had been when he was married but dismissed that question before it left my lips. Some inquiries are simply not in order. He later said that his stay there was work related.

At any rate, I have the cozy days of winter to huddle in with Georgie until spring comes bouncing into place in all its splendor. The jonquils will make themselves the star attraction, and then the roses and hydrangeas will bloom with the good salt air.

Spring on the Cape is captivating. I'll take little back-road jaunts and Georgie will be content to have his paddock to poke around in. There's so much to look forward to. I sometimes question if one life is enough for each of us, and then I wonder if there is more. What is this Heaven we've heard so much about?

For now I am going to enjoy my goat, my painting from Stephen, my knitting, my own good cooking, and the comfort of this humble little house. I am going to make more mittens, scarves, and hats because I like the soft warmth of the wool on my fingers. And when I get the urge to clean out Henry's old desk, I'll do that, too. He was meticulous about his desk and it had quite a jarring when it was moved here. Everything is probably a mess. I've kept it locked and polished. I haven't glanced inside. There is something solemn about another person's sanctuary for personal belongings. I never thought to intrude.

Suzanna told me that she didn't keep any furniture from her former house. Maybe she didn't have anything that held good memories.

I remember holding her one night when she was an infant, lulling her to sleep. I asked Henry what he would do if he were out in a sinking boat with Suzanna. I wanted to know how much he loved her. I asked him if he could save only himself or her, which one would he save. I thought certainly that he would say his daughter's name. He did not. I was heartsick. I asked him why he wouldn't save the life of his child. His answer was that we could have another child, but not another of him. I asked nothing more. I knew then that no matter what ever happened, the tying together of mother and child was greatest. The umbilical cord may be cut, but not severed.

As she grew to a toddler and then a young girl, I watched as they grew closer to one another than they were to me. I felt left aside, but I wanted them to be attached, and now I think I understand why I left Henry to tell her what was right and what was not. I allowed them to bond and leave me in the dust so that their tethering would be strong and reliable. So maybe they didn't do this to me as I've thought for fifty-three years, maybe I instigated the relationship and watched it bloom, content that perhaps Henry would, if asked again who he would save from a sinking boat, the reply would be right.

With Henry gone from both of us, a call to her now and then might be in order. She must miss his persuasive advice, his gentle interference into her life. I've wondered if she moved to California for college and then marriage to escape a father who might pop into her life unannounced if they lived close. I don't think Henry would have done that, but Suzanna might have concerned herself with that possibility.

I doubt that I was a threat. I stayed in the backseat and encouraged the bonding. Without knowing why, until now, I feel certain that had I been a mother who hovered over the growing of our daughter, Henry wouldn't have had the place of honor, providing her with the assurance she needed to grow emotionally fit. I think Henry was better at advice and masterminding guidelines than I could have been. I fly by the seat of my pants, always have, but Henry was a thinker, a planner. I may have given Suzanna the best of me by sitting back and being quiet.

I'll call her now and then. She can shut me down with some excuse if she doesn't want to talk to me, but at least she'll know I am thinking of her. Closing in on eighty-three and she at fifty-four, I would admit to being a late bloomer. But better to bloom late than not at all.

Suzanna

I've done my work, I've fed and walked Casper a dozen times, I've made myself an egg and cheese sandwich and chicken noodle soup from a can, and yet I have not called my children to tell them of their father's situation. Truth be known, I have no idea how to explain because I don't understand it myself.

From what the doctor told me, Glenn and his significant other have parted. Glenn is apparently darkly depressed and feeling lost. I suppose I didn't train him well for this failure. I never said no to him, never indicated that his way was not the only way. He may have expected too much from a new relationship. But he left a family, and now what am I supposed to do? I genuinely do not know how to mend this broken man, and I don't know if I care to.

In the months after he left, I sat in silence for hours, wondering where everything had gone wrong. We had seemed like a good fit. Out of the blue he left, though we'd been drifting apart long before that. I didn't ask him why. I didn't ask him to stay. I was anesthetized.

Now he's asked the doctor to tell me where he is and why. Tall, fit Glenn in a psychiatric hospital in which he admitted himself. I can't imagine his sense of wreckage, expectations in pieces.

I don't know where to go with this. I suppose I need to figure it out. I can't ignore the situation as much as I want to. Or do I? What is this pull to my compassionate side? I've never had to dig this emotion out of myself before, and I'm not sure what's there. I could do him more damage by visiting than I could by staying away. But how can I ignore what's happened to him? I didn't know Glenn was this vulnerable. I thought he was invincible and that nothing could alter that show of strength.

It's at times like that that I miss my father. Dad would have directed me in what I should do. He'd be furious with Glenn for behavior unbecoming to a husband and father. Dad would have given his son-in-law absolute hell for abandonment. As much as I miss Dad, maybe his advice would not be what I need in order to properly cope with this bewildering dilemma.

Until my son opened up to us about being gay, I never knew anyone in that position. I remember feeling shallow, blind for not recognizing my child's state of affairs. I remember thinking that I wasn't as shocked as I might have been. This was his unsolicited demeanor. I think Kira had an idea as well. When she heard the announcement from her parents and brother she said nothing. She didn't seem surprised, but it wasn't long after that when the position in New York called to her.

The truth is, I don't know what to do. I'm an emotional statue. I'm surprised at my thought but maybe what I need to do is call my mother and ask what she would do. She's impassive about life in general, it could be that she would have a sane proposal.

* * *

"Now that I've given you as much information as I understand it from the doctor, what do you make of this? I feel like a hot-air balloon going further and further into the clouds."

I wait for several seconds, hoping my mother will have an immediate response. When she finally speaks, I listen as I may never have before. I need to hear and comprehend what she is capable of relating.

"First, I am very sorry that Glenn is in a damaged state. No one deserves this. Quite sincerely, Suzanna, all I can tell you is what I would do. I wish I had the answer you hoped for about going to Glenn, to being a presence in his healing. I know that I would be called to befriend the father of my child, prop him up rather than push him down. The two of you had more than thirty years together, two children, and a myriad of blended lives.

"The past year must surely have been terrible for you, yet do they hold more importance than the thirty years in which you found contentment and joy? I can't answer that for you. Only you know."

* * *

I hold the phone for a long time after listening to my

mother. Charlene, Sadearah, whoever she is, stated her advice with a calm yet confident voice. I needed that levelheaded sensible statement, feeling wilted just thinking about calling my children. Certainly they had been silently injured by the alteration within their family and they deserve to know the truth.

My father, perceptive as he was, could be more protective of me than reasonable. He definitely would not have taken Glenn's feelings into consideration. Dad would have been angry, he would have stated that Glenn had gotten what he deserved.

I'm not so certain that I didn't feel a bit of that at first. Learning of my husband's rejection was almost satisfying, knowing that he had been injured as he had damaged me. But I don't want to be like my father. I don't want to abandon someone who at one time did mean something to me.

Sadearah

I am feeling both distraught and disheartened regarding my son-in-law. I watched him from afar with his children, appearing to be caring wholeheartedly for them. And I was aware of how he and Suzanna enjoyed their enriched lives in sunny California, seeking culture and happy times as a family. He tried. It must have been terribly difficult for him to pretend. It had to have been important to him to blend in, to be a good husband and father, and not to be revealed until he couldn't take the deception any longer. At times I've tried to understand this, but as a mother my instinct was to be angry with him for what he did to Suzanna.

Now he has made himself ill with the collapse of his new life and the familiar longing for his relationship with my daughter. He needs her. I don't know if she can handle this, but yes, he needs her.

I will trust that Suzanna will determine what's best. In the meanwhile, I have things to keep myself busy. I've made a list which includes thoroughly cleaning out sweet Georgie's shed, washing my kitchen floor with my nice new mop, and I'm finally going to get Henry's desk unlocked and neatly arranged.

I don't know why I haven't wanted to interfere with how my husband had organized his life on paper, but it's a shame for that little desk not to see the light of day and be neatened after eight years of neglect. I worry about being invasive, that my fingers will touch what Henry treasured, special notes and cards from his family, his journal. I worry that I am an uninvited intruder, about what I may find, yet my intentions are strong. I will clean the shed and kitchen first, but in a day or two, or maybe next week, the desk.

* * *

Georgie has been mostly content here with me in the kitchen, yet on days not terribly cold he's enjoyed a little poking about in his paddock. It's plain nonsense to make an animal feel the penetrating cold when they don't have to, and Georgie is welcome right here in the warmth. I talk to him and he listens, usually chewing on a clump of hay or a slice or two of apple. At any rate, the shed has been cleaned and I'm sure that come spring he'll welcome being in his own space.

My kitchen has the aroma of hay and also of good cooking. It's not a bad combination, earthy and comforting. Now I sit in my chair and stare at Henry's desk. There's something prohibitive about that piece of furniture, yet it calls to me. When I've finished my tea, I will unlock the slanted top and I will make the contents orderly. I will remove everything and dust as I polish the

214

interior. This will be my tribute to Henry all the while making my blood pressure rise. I have never touched anything inside his desk, not that I was forbidden. It's just that I like my own privacy and I respect that others do as well.

My cup is empty and it's time to stop procrastinating and get to my planned duty. The small key was always in the blue tin among a stack of books. It feels foreign in my hand, yet for the first time, I realize that's it's quite ornate, a pretty little piece of brass.

Inserting it into the keyhole I feel a chill, almost the sense that my touch has drawn Henry to my side. I smile and shed tears at the same time. So much of him was caring and considerate. And yet, for so many years, decades, I've wondered about the woman he loved before he married me.

So here in cubby holes he has tucked receipts from items purchased as far back as when we were first wed. He even has the rental agreement on our first apartment together where we lived for just over a year before purchasing the Jamaica Plain house. And there are other receipts and contracts, neatly folded and tucked in together for easy acquisition. None of this is needed now, yet Henry saved these things and so will I.

In spite of having been jostled about in the move, the interior does not seem badly disturbed. I probably could have left it alone, but even an old desk, used to being respected and helpful, might like an airing and a glimpse of light. So here I am, giving it the regard it deserves.

Fastened with a brown string is a stack of what seems to be cards and letters. I'll take a glance through them, some look like cards I gave to him for his birthday, an anniversary, and a few are from Suzanna. Among these are notes and cards from Henry's mother. I'm not sure she liked me all that much, she was a talker and I was not. Nevertheless, Henry treasured these pieces enough to keep them tied together, like a family.

His journal rests flat, tucked in back of the writing surface. I look at it and wonder if I should leave it alone. Staring at its marbled colored cover, I wonder what I might read if I open that book. My hands are on the wood, the tips of my fingers on the journal. I have dusted around it, careful not to expose the paper to the oily polish.

With a decision to be brave about this, I pull the journal toward me and think about having another cup of tea. No. I'm procrastinating. I open the cover and turn to the first page which holds the original handwritten receipt. This was something started before he met me. He purchased this life record in Harvard Square. I smile thinking how Henry liked lovely covers and good quality paper.

I move from the first page which recorded notes about essays he was planning to write for Western Civilization class, and glance at the next few pages containing scribbles about his friends, a group I knew of, John, Max, Brendan, and Jack. He mentioned how they'd enjoyed a basketball game together, a bit of street hockey on the college campus. He mentioned where in Boston they sold the best hot dogs and the best cannoli and rum slices. I smile, reliving his spoken words to me about these events and places.

A few pages further I find harmless comments about girls on campus, their long legs and short skirts, blondes versus brunettes. Nothing about light brown headed girls, like me. Again I smile.

It is on the thirty-fourth page that I find what I was not searching for. He wrote:

Today is Charly's and my second wedding anniversary and a child is about to become an integral part of us. (I shed tears recalling that he sometimes called me Charly rather than Charlene when we were young.)

I think back to the agony I put myself through when Patricia denied my proposal and seemed almost disrespected for my hopes in being together. Thankfully, she knew better than I. I cannot imagine a more perfect union than this magnificent alliance with my darling wife. Charlene, my Charly, is perfection, the most beautiful female I have ever rested eyes upon. I willingly surrender my heart and soul to her on this dear anniversary as well as forever. Forever won't be nearly long enough.

The front of my shirt and my face are drenched in tears. I had no idea that Henry cared for me this deeply, and to know that *her* name was not Suzanna means the world to me.

Another time I will further peruse the remaining pages. I am both sorrowful and joyful, overwhelmed with this sweet discovery. My husband loved me more than the one who got away.

* * *

The desk is gleaming with having received a deserved polishing. Georgie is here staring at me, I think because I have yet to turn on the TV which he stares at as he chews. And I am thinking of what I want for my dinner. I am so filled with gratefulness in finding Henry's written words, I am not sure I have room within my body for food.

I believe I will comb my silver strands, change into a nightdress and robe, then maybe I'll have a nice baked potato with scallions, sour cream, and butter. Georgie might savor that as well.

The end.

Sadearah is based on a woman I observed while on the open sea from Boothbay Harbor, Maine to Monhegan Island. She was silver-haired, with silvery eyelashes and brows, and she possessed more facial wrinkles than anyone I had ever seen. She was the most beautiful human and, without knowing her name, I invented Sadearah because I thought it was deserved. I heard her speaking to a stranger on the boat – she mentioned having goats.